Whose BABY?

MELISSA JONES

Whose Baby?

Copyright © 2015 by Melissa Jones

ISBN 978-9839483-7-7

Library of Congress Control Number 2015934866

Published by
Rapier Publishing Company
360 W. Main Street, Ste #1
Dothan, Alabama 36301

www.rapierpublishing.com
Facebook: www.rapierpublishing@gmail.com
Twitter: rapierpublishing@rapierpub

Printed in the United States of America

Book Cover Design: Drew Key (Kew-Koncepts)

Book Layout: Rapture Graphics

Dedication

This book is dedicated in loving memory of our daughter

Kai M. Jones
(1996-2011)

I have always believed in God. I have always believed that Jesus died and rose on the third day. What I believed was never the problem. It was my walk with God that was questionable. As a child, my parents told my sisters and me that we should go to church because it is key to our spiritual growth and going to Bible study would help us understand God's Word for ourselves. They told us that once we accepted Christ into our hearts and began to walk with the Lord, our attitudes, the way we thought, and talked would change. Well, they were right! Before my life turned into a soap opera with more drama than you could ever imagine, I went to church and Bible study. However, it was not until my life was turned upside down, that I finally can say that I know what it means to walk with the Lord and to rely on Him for guidance, strength, and forgiveness.

Mackenzie Clay

Chapter 1

My name is Dr. MacKenzie Dianne Clay. I am six-foot one. I weigh about one- hundred and seventy pounds with a twenty-four inch waistline and plenty of junk in my trunk. I am in excellent physical condition. I work out daily to help relieve stress. My complexion is a caramel color much like a caramel candied apple, it's completely flawless. My eyes are dark brown and slightly slanted. My brows are so thick; I have to keep them arched. My hair is shoulder length, bronze in color, with natural big curls. I probably would put one in the mind of Vanessa Williams, the first black Miss America, but with a nicer rear section. I have been accused of thinking that I am all that. The truth is, I am shy and can be standoffish from people that I don't know.

I live in Seattle, Washington. I am a psychiatrist at The Loving Hearts Counseling Center, a non-profit psychiatric foundation in the Seattle area. The center provides counseling services to all women, regardless of their ability to pay. After I graduated from college, I chose to live in Seattle, Washington, and take this job after my high school boyfriend broke my heart. He lives in my hometown of Carmel, Indiana. I just could not bear seeing him every day, especially after what he did to me. Any who! Let's get to the story.

As I mentioned earlier, my walk with God had always been questionable. I guess my walk was questionable because I simply didn't know what I was supposed to do after I got saved.

I grew up in the church, but never had a real understanding of what church was about because no one told me anything except to accept Jesus Christ into your heart, be baptized, go to the Lord's house every Sunday, and you will go to heaven. I would see women shouting and crying, and falling out and did not understand what it was all about. When I would ask my mom what was going on, I was told "She was slain by the spirit." Ooookay. What does that mean? I was some kind of confused.

I attended Columbia University in New York immediately after high school, where I earned my undergraduate degree in social work by the age of twenty-one. I continued my quest for my graduate degree in Counseling Psychology, which I earned by the age of twenty-three. Since it didn't appear that I was getting married anytime soon, much to my dismay, I continued with school until I earned my doctorate of philosophy degree in Counseling. I accomplished all of this by the ripe old age of thirty. Between the ages of twenty-three and twenty-five, I also completed a Specialist degree in Counseling. During this time span, I had to complete eighteen hundred hours of direct counseling experience with patients while being supervised by a licensed professional counselor for three consecutive years while I worked toward my doctoral degree. Whew! Completing high school, four years of undergraduate work, two years for my Master's Degree, two years for my Specialist Degree, and then three years for my Doctoral Degree…I am tired!! It was a lot, but it was worth it when it was all over.

My parents had always stressed the importance of an education to my sisters and me. They said I needed to get all the degrees I was going to get before I got married and started having children. My mom would say, "Baby, momma wants you to know that the tall, dark, handsome and wealthy man that you've read about in books, is there…in the books. They are fairy tales. You need to always be able to take care of yourself. Now, if that man does appear and is wealthy and can give you your heart's desire and loves you completely, that's a blessing. But in case he can't, you will be able to have a roof over your head, food in your mouth, and a good job." She was right. I needed to be sure that I could take care of me no matter what.

When I moved to the Seattle area, my mom told me to make sure I find a church home. Well, I found one, The Holiness of God Church of the Living Word, a non-denominational church. It didn't matter if you were Catholic, Baptist, or Methodist, or however you were identifying yourself, you could come to this church. The preacher always delivered the Word; he didn't care what kind of spin you put on it after he delivered it. The name in itself told me that this would be the place where I would find the answers to my questions. The members were very nice and welcoming. I knew I had found my church home when I met Alondra Venezuela. She was a very attractive young lady that seemed to have it together. She reminded me of my friend Carmen from back home and she was also a friend of Lorna's, whom I met in college, so she had to be cool. She made sure that she spoke to me every Sunday. One Sunday, after four months of attending the church, as the pastor was speaking, I looked around at the congregation, and thought to myself, "We need some eligible men up in this camp." I had been attending this church for months and the pickings here were null and void. It had to get better.

It was approaching the last Sunday in the month of August when I started to plan my activities for the following month. I have always tried to be organized. For someone as busy as I am, if I didn't have a calendar app on my iPad and iPhone, I was going to miss something. Even with these devices, I still some-times missed a couple of things, but that should be expected, right? Perusing my calendar, I discovered that it was time for my annual physical. Oh joy! It is definitely not on the top of my list of things that I enjoy doing, but I know that it is a necessary part of life for women. Since I was new to the area, I had no idea of who to see so I called my friend Lorna Whyte. I met her at Columbia and she is one of the reasons that I moved to Seattle. She also took me to her church, which I love so dearly. She uses Dr. Celeste Morgan. She gave me her telephone number and I called and scheduled an appointment. Dr. Morgan came highly recommended. She was the only black female gynecologist in the area.

On Tuesday morning I went to see Dr. Morgan. When I arrived at her office, I was quite impressed. With her being black and owning her own practice, I expected to see certain things like scuffed walls where women had allowed their bad children to kick it or draw on them. I expected to see a small waiting room of about fifteen women; all with a nine o'clock appointment like I had experienced at other gynecological/obstetrician offices that I had visited in the past. They would sit and speculate (gossip) about why they thought a particular person was there. Oh! I had a salon flash back. I digress. To my surprise, this wasn't true. The office was tastefully decorated with chocolate leather furniture and expensive black art hanging on what appeared to be freshly painted taupe colored walls. There were also hand crafted high back chairs that were so comfortable I'd just as soon stay there and she come out and speak with me where I sat. All that was waiting in the back was a cold room and a hard table and a set of stirrups. Ew!

There were only two women in the waiting room, me and another woman. She was very sullen in mood. She was about five-foot eleven inches, very beautiful with hazel eyes, the saddest hazel eyes I have ever seen. She sat reading a pamphlet about the grief you experience when you lose a baby. My heart immediately went out to her. I have no idea what it is like to lose a baby and prayed that I would never find out. After I finished filling out all the necessary paper work, I sat and waited to see the doctor.

In about ten minutes, I was called in. After the preliminaries (the undressing and the dreaded cup), Dr. Morgan came in. When she walked, in I thought she looked familiar. No bells went off or red flags went up, but she had a familiarity about her. Anyway, she ran some tests, asked how long I had been in the area; you know, the usual stuff a doctor might ask when you are a new patient. I thought her questions were somewhat invasive, but hey I was there for a gynecological visit, how much more invasive could she have been. The visit went well, and I was told that I was in good health; however, one of the tests revealed that I had a low blood iron level. She prescribed some vitamins and stated that she wanted to check my iron level again in about six months and that I needed to schedule a follow-up appointment. I didn't think much about it. I made the follow-up appointment and went home.

I continued to attend The Holiness of God Church of the Living Word and enjoyed it most of the time. There was one woman there that intrigued me. Her name was Mrs. Kingsley. She would sometimes pray for individuals when they came to the altar. I had never spoken with her, but for some reason I feared her. The people that she would touch and pray for would cry and carry on. I didn't know what she was telling them, but I did not want to hear anything that would make me carry on like that. She had a peace about her that I admired, I was just afraid that she would tell me that something was wrong in my life and that I needed to get myself together. Well, I already knew that, I just did not want her to know it too.

Mrs. Kingsley was considered the mother of the church. She had seen so much in her life. She had buried both her parents and two siblings. She was married for thirty-five years when her husband died of complications related to diabetes. She was unable to have children, so she had no living family. She was about seventy-five years old and always appeared to be in a good mood. She would always say, "By the grace of the living God, I am here and I am good." It didn't seem possible that one person could have so much loss and still be that happy. Maybe she had a special connection to God? I didn't know, but she was an awesome woman that was loved by everyone in the church. I wasn't quite ready to meet her yet, but I knew I would meet her one day and that we would be friends.

After seven months of attending the church, it happened. It was the fourth Sunday in April. We were all dressed casually. I had on a tangerine linen suit. The skirt touched the bottom of my knee. The blouse was silk and tangerine and lime in color. I wore tangerine sling back heels that made my calves look tight! Hey I worked out, I liked to flaunt them. I just had to be subtle about it in church. My girl Lorna had on a turquoise linen pant suit, a turquoise and blue linen blouse and matching sandals. She also wore earrings, a choker, and a matching bracelet to complete her ensemble. They were custom made. My girl was nothing but the truth. As we were enjoying praise and worship, in walked the finest brother I had ever seen. All I could think was "Good Lawd, that brother is fine! Come over here and sit with me baby!" Then I caught myself and said "Lord, forgive me for looking at that man like that in your house. But Lord, that brother is fine!" Lorna and I looked at each other and shook our heads and said "Hmmm" under our breath. Anybody that fine should not be allowed to enter the house of the Lord by himself. He sat on the third pew on the right side of the church. Wouldn't you know it; we were on the left side on the seventh row of the church.

During the service I was watching that man so hard I don't know what the pastor was saying. I doubt if Lorna knew either.

That nut starting writing me notes about how fine that man was. Picture it, a man about six-feet four inches tall with a six pack and guns like The Rock and a face with dimples like Lamman Rucker, the actor who plays Will on Tyler Perry's comedy sitcom, "Meet the Browns". No, I couldn't see his six pack, but the way he was looking from head to toe and working those clothes, I knew he had to have one. His skin appeared smooth and creamy like chocolate pudding. I normally don't like pudding, but for him, I was willing to make an exception! His hair was closely cut like Maxwell, the R & B singer, but it had the potential for fingers to be intertwined in it at just the right moment. "Why is it so hot in here all of a sudden?" Lorna touched my arm and snapped me back to reality. The last note Lorna wrote stated, "Girl, he might be alright, I do not see any gold teeth from here." I got so tickled; I thought I was going to have to leave the sanctuary. I shook for almost a minute as Lorna sat there pretending she didn't know what was going on. She was good at that and I know this, so why I would read a note from her, I have no idea. After I regained my composure, I started thinking of how I was going to get to meet this tall glass of chocolate milk before the other single women could get to him. Then I snapped back to my senses. I am quite shy in nature so approaching this good looking man really was not an option for me. Anyway as you may have guessed, I did not get a chance to get within fifty feet of him after the service. I was a little too far away from him to casually bump into him without stepping on a few sisters in the process, so I let it go. Lorna and I parted company after the service. She was going to lunch with her boyfriend Khalil and I knew I was not feeling watching their love story today. As I was getting into my white C-Class Coupe Mercedes (yes, the agency was non-profit, but I have also consultative jobs to get want I needed and wanted), a deep voice behind me said, "Excuse me, I am new in town, do you know of any good restaurants in the area?" I said to myself, "Girl, don't act crazy. Just keep your cool and answer the man's question." I turned around all sexy like, and didn't see anyone. All of sudden I heard the voice again. "Excuse me, I am new in town, do you know of any good restaurants in the area?" I looked down and there he was. I saw a brother about five feet four inches tall smiling up at me. I looked at him and thought to myself, "I know this li'l short man is not trying to push up on me?" If he was standing any closer, he would have been able to tell me if I needed to clean my nose. As I was about to answer his shortness, tall and good looking walked up behind him. Those beautiful pink lips all covered with a nicely trimmed mustache spoke. I don't know what he said; all I could do was watch his lips move. After I snapped out of my trance I heard him say "Jamal, who's your beautiful friend?" I almost wet my pants. I wanted to stand on top of Jamal and say "I'll be who you want me to be baby!" I introduced myself as MacKenzie Dianne Clay. Tall and oh my goodness! was named Preston, Preston Stone. Up close and personal, he was actually six-foot six, about two-hundred and fifteen pounds, and oh my, my, my, is all I can say about the rest. If I described this brother in any more detail, you would probably come through this book and take him from me and I am not having it!

After we exchanged our pleasantries, we said our good byes and off he went. Come to think of it, I never did answer Jamal's question. Now that was a trip. I had all that fineness in my face and I did nothing! I couldn't believe it. There must have been something wrong with that brother. I know he had to have known I was definitely interested in him even if I didn't say it. I thought he was interested in me by the way he flashed that beautiful white smile at me. Oh well. There is always next Sunday.

Three months had passed and Preston had not returned to church. No wonder he did not ask for my number, he must have been from out of town. Oh well, he sure was nice eye candy. Any who, I remembered it was time for me to go for my follow up with Dr. Morgan. When I went in for my follow up visit, she stated that I was doing well and that my iron level was eleven, close to what was considered normal for a woman of my age. Hemoglobin levels are considered normal when they range from 12 to 16 for a woman my age according to Dr. Morgan. She did encourage me to continue to take the vitamins until my hemoglobin level reached above twelve. She then asked the typical question that all thirty year old, single women are asked, "When are you planning to get married and have children?" After I snickered, I confirmed that I needed a man to accomplish that task. Dr. Morgan stated "You know there is a way to have children that is not the typical way." I gave her a look of…what? She handed me a brochure about in vitro fertilization. We both giggled. I asked Dr. Morgan where she attended church. She stated that she had not found one because she not been in the area very long. She had been in Seattle for less than two years and most of her time had been trying to get her business off the ground. I invited her to come to Holiness of God. She stated that she just might. I provided her with the address and directions of how to get to the church and then I was gone.

It was the first Sunday in October and we were preparing for communion when the pastor asked that everyone move to the front of the church until all the pews were filled. I was sitting on the second row. Lorna was not there this particular Sunday because she was out of town on business. After I placed my things under the pew making room for anyone who wanted to join me on the row, a wonderful fragrance filled my nostrils. The scent was familiar and inviting. Then the thought came to mind that it was probably Deacon Frittle. He was always grinning at me and saying "Girl, if I was twenty years younger" and I would always think to myself, "You would still be a hundred years old and too old for me!" As I lifted my head and prepared to put on my Deacon Frittle smile, I just sat there with my mouth open. You are absolutely right. It was Preston. He smiled very sweetly.

I returned the smile and then turned back to look at pastor for further instructions. I started sweating and my heart was racing. "Lord why did you let him sit beside me? Why are you torturing me Lord? I am trying to be a good girl, but you are trying me!" As the communion tray reached me, I took my cup and passed it to Preston. He looked very serious as he took his cup and that made me feel good that he was familiar with this practice.

After about a month of seeing each other at church and smiling and saying our cordial hellos and making small talk, Preston asked me to lunch. We went to a nice restaurant and had a really pleasant time. You know I eyed him intensely. He had the most beautiful white teeth. Yes, I was all in his mouth. Who wants someone all up in your face with a ragged grill and some humming breath? He was quite entertaining, and had a sweet spirit about him. All I could think was "Lord is he the one?" After lunch we went to the park. He pushed me on the swing and picked wild flowers for me. Yes, black people engage in this behavior. LOL! How could he be more perfect? As he pushed me in the swing, a little girl about the age of four came up and attempted to get into the swing next to me. Preston and I smiled as she struggled. He then walked over to help her into the swing. Oh man! She was absolutely gorgeous! She had the blackest hair that was braided neatly and beaded at the ends. She had the cutest lime green Capri warm up suit completed with white Keds that were spotless, at least for now. She had an angelic smile and always responded yes ma'am or yes sir or no ma'am or no sir. Preston was so gentle with our little swing mate. After about ten minutes I wondered why her mom had not come over. I looked around and didn't see anyone. I started to ask her questions. When asked she stated her name was Millicent and that she was four. When Preston asked where her mother was, she just smiled and said she's at home. I thought to myself, I know her mom has not bumped her head and allowed this little girl to be out here alone. She indicated that she didn't live far. We decided to walk her home. She was very smart and took us to where she lived. By the time we reached her house, a young woman came running out of her house almost hysterical. As it turns out, our little friend had asked her mom to take her to the park. Millicent became inpatient and decided to go alone while her mom was taking a shower. She had just realized that Millicent was gone. She thanked us and took Millicent into the house. Although her mom was praising God that she was okay, I think little miss was going to have flashbacks every time she thought of going to the park alone because she was about to get the spanking of her life.

After we arrived at my house, Preston said good night, gave me a warm embrace, kissed me on the cheek and he was gone. Ump, ump, ump. What a man! I couldn't believe that he was true. Then it happened. An awful thought came to my mind. What if he's a psycho? Fine don't mean jack when you are running for your life. Can you see me running from ol' boy thinking "Boy you sure look good! Look at those muscles ripple as you're swinging that heavy axe at me!" "Lord, if he is not the one, please reveal it in the name of Jesus!" For the first time since our initial meeting, I got scared. I got really scared.

I often envisioned being in love. Because I am a hopeless romantic, all the things I envisioned about being in love do not center on things that can be purchased but rather on things like sending sweet text messages to each other, holding hands whenever we are together, staring into each other's eyes and being oblivious to anyone else, except each other. He would walk into the room and I would not be able to concentrate on anything but him holding me and telling me how much he loved me and me him. We would finish each other's sentences. If we argued, we would be physically ill until we have made up. We would then get married and live happily ever after. Does this sound like a fairy tale or what? It could happen! Work with me people!

After we dated for about one month I was convinced that he was okay. I did not sense anything was wrong. Shouldn't I if there was? Now my mommy told me that when things aren't right, a little voice would tell you. I looked up toward the ceiling and said, "Voice, if you have anything to say, say it now or forever hold your peace." Nothing! I waited a little while longer, nothing. Well I guess everything is good. Whenever we went out, it was always the same thing at the end of the date, a warm embrace, a kiss on the cheek and he was gone. I wondered for a minute if the man was gay. Oh Lord! Don't tell me the brother is undercover! On the down low! Is he married? Noooooooooooo! "MacKenzie calm down! Can you just slow your roll?" Okay. Everything is fine. Just relax girl.

Well, as it turns out he was not a psycho, it was even worse; he was the most romantic, sweet-talking man I had ever met. If we get into a compromising position, will I be able to resist him? As he gazed into my eyes and held me close, I was thinking "Okay girl, don't jump on him! Then a small voice said, "You are moving too fast. He needs to leave before you do something you will regret." All I could think was, "If I let this man leave here now, I know I am going to regret it, but definitely for a different reason." We shared a passionate kiss and looked deeply into each other eyes. There goes that voice again, but this time I did not hear it, he did. He pulled away. He said as he stood back and released me with a sigh of regret, "I had better leave." My flesh was saying "You ain't got to go nowhere!" My mind was saying "Stop tripping! You know he needs to leave!" So I walked him to the door and he kissed me on the cheek and he was gone.

We carried on like this for about six months. He would come to my house, things would begin to heat up and then he would leave. I was sure glad that he had some will power, because I had zero! I was so in love that reason was hard to hear when it came to what I felt for him. We were very physically attracted to one another, which was more than obvious. We talked about intimacy on a few occasions. We talked about how we felt and that although he wanted to be intimate with me, he knew it would not be right and that he wanted our relationship to be based on true love and not lust. He wanted our relationship to be blessed, so he was going to go slow. I was so touched, I almost cried. When I think about that moment, I almost cry. I was so accustomed to having to fight men off literally, going Mike Tyson on a dude because of his aggressiveness. No ear biting though, they may have liked it and thought it was foreplay. This man just could not be real. It had to be a dream that I was going to wake up from. My thoughts then wondered as to why he never stayed past 8:00 and why I never went to his house. I know you guys are saying "You big dummy! You know why! He has a wife! Duh?" Naw, stop playing! This is a Christian man. After all, he has joined our church and is very involved in helping the young men get themselves together by teaching them how to handle themselves when they face peer pressure. Preston is trying to do right by me and I appreciate it. Just stay with me okay? There are men out there like Preston, really!

Like I said, after about six months of this, Preston popped the question. No, it wasn't will you go away with me for the weekend? It was the real deal Holyfield, "Will you marry me?" I could not believe it. This man is asking me to marry him. What do I truly know about him? What does he know about me? I have not met his family. I don't even know where this man lives! I don't know what he does for a living. Does he even have a job? All these thoughts were rushing through my mind. What do I say? My heart was racing. Every ounce of me was screaming, "Say no!" I looked at him and couldn't say anything for a minute. Then I heard the word yes come out of my mouth. The next thing I know, I have a two-caret marquee cut diamond on my finger. I am getting married.

I asked Preston about his family. I know, fine time to ask this question after I have already said I would marry the man. He stated that his parents were deceased and that he was an only child. I asked him why he had never taken me to his home. He simply stated that he wanted to be sure that I loved him for him before he could show me where he lived and other things about his life. Oh Lord! Good looking doesn't have anywhere decent to live and he is embarrassed about where he lives. Come to think of it, his car is about eight years old. Bless his heart. That means that he doesn't have much money. He should know that those things don't matter to me. But it does settle the question of where we are going to live-my house.

I asked him what he thought about having children. He looked into my eyes almost as if he were looking through me. He then stated that he wanted to have only one child. I thought that was a little odd especially because he was an only child and he knew how lonely that could be. But he insisted that he only wanted one. I guess that was okay. It's not like he was asking for seven. I could live with one. I thought to myself "I am so lucky. Thank you Lord for this FINE man!"

That night I could not get to sleep. So much excitement had happened that day. First I called my mom and dad to give them the news. They were speechless. My mom said, "How is it that are you planning to marry some man I have never laid eyes on? Is he a Christian? Does he drink? Does he have a good job? Where is he from? She just kept firing off questions, and I realized that there were questions that I could not answer. I started to answer her questions, but my telephone clicked indicating that I had another call. It was Lorna. Thank you Lord for call waiting and caller ID. I told my mom I had to go and clicked over very quickly.

"Lorna, girl!" "What? What's wrong?" Lorna asked. "Lorna… Preston asked me to marry him." "What???!!!!!!!!!!!!!!!" She squealed so loud on the phone, I almost dropped it. "You heard me, Preston asked me to marry him." "What did you say?" asked Lorna. "I said yes." "Hold up, I know that man did not ask you to marry him and you are acting like you are marrying Deacon Frittle?" said Lorna. "I mean, I said yes!!! Ok!! I burst into laughter at the thought of me marrying Deacon Frittle. I shared with her all the questions that my mom had asked and that I could not answer. "Well, ask him! How hard can that be? Girl, I do not believe you have been dating this man all this time and do not know the answers to these questions. What do y'all talk about when you are together? You do talk, right?" asked Lorna. "Girl, don't make me come through this telephone. Of course we talk…some." LOL (Laughing out loudly)! responded Mackenzie. I just never asked those questions because I just imagined what he did and it became my reality. What am I going to do?" "You are going to calm down and get answers. Don't worry, as long as he is not a stripper, gay, or doing something illegal, you should be okay. Relax, girl. You are getting married!" "Yes, I am. Thank you girl for keeping it real with me, I'll let you know what I find out." "Cool. Just remember one thing; I do not want to wear some big green fru fru dress in your wedding!" We both laughed and hung up. I felt much better. My girl can always make me feel better and see the positive in things.

When I finally fell asleep, I had a dream. I had had this dream before, but couldn't figure out what it meant. This particular night, the dream went to another level. I saw a woman in a mask. For the most part the dreams had no sound. This particular time, the dream was loud and in living color. A voice was saying that this woman is not as she appears. "Look beyond the mask." The voice repeated itself, "Look beyond the mask." Go figure?

Chapter 2

I had always been unsure of myself for as long as I could remember. I grew tall very quickly. By the age of ten I was already 5' 6" tall. I appeared to be all arms and legs. I was always the tallest girl in my class. I was often called string bean, bones, or skinny minny. The only friend I had was Carmen. She was just as tall and just as skinny as I was.

It was time to pick teams for kick ball and as usual I was hoping I would get picked, but it didn't look like it was going to happen, again. Instead, I got picked on by a boy named Nathan. I was just about to cry and run away from the playground when Carmen stepped in. Just as Nathan was about to call me another name….POW! Carmen punched him in the nose so hard it knocked him flat on his butt. Then she stood over him and asked, "What were you about to call her?" This act of bravery by Carmen caused me to feel empowered. I felt so empowered that I stood beside Carmen, both of us now towering over Nathan. I repeated Carmen's question, "What were you about to call me?" By this time all the kids who usually stood around and laughed as Nathan picked on me had already retreated. Nathan got up with his tail between his legs and ran to tell the teacher. We were in the fifth grade. Carmen introduced herself to me and we started to hang out together on the playground. From that day forward no one talked about or heckled me again. To think Carmen stood up for me when I couldn't stand up for myself. After that day I didn't ever feel scared to stand up for myself again. Even if Carmen wasn't at school, I was still able to stand my ground even if it meant I had to put someone on the ground. Fighting is never the answer and it didn't feel good after the one time that I had to do it, but unfortunately it was unavoidable. Carmen and I remained friends throughout middle and high school. We started hanging out less and less as we grew older and discovered boys, but I knew that I could count on Carmen and Carmen knew she could count on me.

Due to my shyness, I had always attracted boys that thought I was weak or an easy target. The boys would act as if they were interested in me until they realized how shy I was and that I was not as easy as they thought. Once they discovered this, they would move on. Justin Franks started to talk to me during physical education class. We were required to dress out and then meet our teacher outside at the track located on the east side of the school building. The teacher would call the roll and then we could do whatever we wanted as long as we stayed in the designated area of the track. I liked to run and so did Justin so we would often run together. He was easy to talk to and never tried to hit on me. I definitely wanted him to, but we were just friends. I guessed that would have to do. One day after school, Justin and I decided to go running around the neighborhood near the school. We were trying out for the cross-country team and needed all the practice we could get so we decided to follow the course that the school had mapped out for all students practicing to make the team. After we had run for about a mile, I stepped in a hole, lost my footing, and fell. Justin helped me up. I insisted upon trying to walk back to campus, but there was no way that was going to happen. I had sprained my ankle. Justin motioned for me to climb onto his back. I wasn't hearing it. I insisted on trying to walk. He gave me a choice, either I would climb onto his back and allow him to carry me back to school that way or he would lift me and carry me the way firemen do hoisted across his shoulder. I decided that this was a losing battle and finally climbed unto his back. I remained quiet as we trekked back to the school. Once we arrived he lowered me onto the ground. "You really didn't have to do that Justin." "What was I supposed to do, leave you on the side of the road and run back for help? I would never have forgiven myself if something had happened to you. I would never leave someone I love behind." After an awkward pause I asked, "You love me?" "Yes. You don't think I have been hanging out with you for the past two months just because you would run with me, do you?" Justin asked. "I guess not. Justin…I love you too." He took me home and asked if I would be his girlfriend. I said yes and we shared our first kiss as boyfriend and girlfriend. We would be inseparable for the next two years. I was a fifteen-year old high school sophomore madly in love. Life was great!

I was hopelessly in love with him and knew that this would be the man that I would marry. He was so sweet, good looking, and a lot of fun to be around. During the two years that we dated, he often talked about getting married. He wanted to love and protect me. That's what I loved most about him. He reminded me of my dad, loving and protective. I thought that was what I wanted and needed in a husband. My dad had always told me how beautiful and smart I was and that I didn't need a man to take care of me. I needed to be able to take care of myself before I ever considered getting married. Besides, I was only seventeen and that was the last thing I needed to be thinking about anyway, but it was fun to think of the possibilities. I just made sure I didn't tell my dad what I am thinking.

I planned to go to college after high school. Initially I thought about being a nurse. I had always wanted to help others and I thought that would be a great way to do it. My mother was a nurse and she absolutely loved her job. I wanted that same job satisfaction one day. Justin had other plans. His dad worked and his mom stayed at home. Justin wanted a woman to do what his mom did. He wanted his wife to stay at home while he went out and made the money. She would take care of the babies, and wait patiently for him to come home from work each day with a hot meal waiting on the table. I was not that girl. I insisted that I was going to college and that I was going to have a career. I wanted children and to take care of Justin, but I needed a career, and that was something that I was not willing to give up. I considered Justin's way of thinking to be that of a Neanderthal. The things I once loved and found cute about him, were now starting to annoy me and vice versa.

I went to Columbia University in the fall. I was so excited. I couldn't wait to explore that huge campus. I knew attending a college as prestigious as Columbia would be a challenge, but it was one that I was looking forward to having. I hoped that Justin would understand what I wanted and needed and that things would eventually work out between us so that we could have our fairy tale marriage after all.

After being away from home for four months, I was ready to go home. Justin and I were writing to each other once a week. Every other week we talked on the telephone, but I could tell things were changing. I couldn't go home before Christmas break because money was tight. I had been awarded some scholarship money and mom and dad had been saving for my college education since my birth, the same as they did for all of their children, but I knew I had to spend money wisely. I knew I needed to get home to see Justin. I hoped that our separation had given us time to think about our relationship and miss each other enough that things would be better than they were before I left for Columbia in September. In my heart, I knew differently.

As soon as I got home and was settled in I called Justin to let him know that I was home. He sounded like he was excited that I was home, but when I asked him to come over to my house to see me, he said that it wasn't a good idea because I had just gotten home and should spend the first night at home with my family. I thought it was sweet, but I couldn't believe that we had been apart since September and he wasn't rushing over to see me. I was disappointed, but agreed it was the best thing to do. I hung up and called Carmen. Carmen had decided to live at home so that she could work and go to college locally. Carmen was ready for her friend to come home so that we could catch up. She was at work when I called. She had left a message for me that she was getting off late, but she would call me tomorrow so we could make plans to hang out. Justin came by the next day just as we had planned. I was so excited. We embraced and kissed and it felt like all was right with the world. I felt better about our relationship. I thought to myself that I was worried for nothing. He loved me as much as he always did.

We discussed how we would spend the next two weeks together balancing time for ourselves and time for me to be with my family and friends. Justin had decided not to go away to college. He always had a love for cars, so he went to the local technical college to start working on becoming a certified mechanic. He had done well in school during the fall semester. He hoped that someday he would have his own business and he was definitely headed in the right direction. He knew it meant hard work, but he was willing to do what it took because it was important to him.

Justin shared all he had been up to since the last time that we had talked while I was away at school. I was always excited about Justin someday owning his own business and being Mrs. Justin Franks. I would listen attentively and encouraged him to follow his dream. He didn't always reciprocate. When I shared how school was going so far, Justin didn't appear all that interested. I was a little irritated about his behavior, but I decided to let it slide. Any other time I would have asked him what his problem was, but I wanted to make good use of the time that we had together because I would be going to back to school soon.

We had a good time hanging out the majority of the day, but I started to sense that there was something that he wasn't saying. I had not always been one to speak my mind. I could when it came to Justin. This time my gut told me to let it go. We parted ways around 6:00 that evening. He was headed home for dinner. No sooner than I got into the house, there was a knock at the back door. It was Justin. This can't be good I thought to myself.

Justin motioned for me to sit down on the steps that led back into the house. Justin started by saying that he loved me very much and that he would always love me, BUT he wasn't sure that he was in love with me anymore. We wanted different things in life and he just couldn't go on pretending that he was happy with the way things were going between us. And that was that. Who did he think that he was kidding? This was probably what he had been planning to say all day. I just sat there stunned staring at him. I had hoped that he would understand that my dreams were important and support them, but he never did. In fact, he continued by saying that he came to see me hoping that he would feel differently about us when he saw me, but he just didn't. I just continued to sit and look at him and said nothing. I got up, turned away from him, and went back into the house. I didn't allow my tears to fall until the door separated us.

I cried. I started thinking that maybe I should just forget about school and come home and marry Justin and just be the housewife and mother Justin wanted me to be for him. After all, with all the guys who had tried to date me, he was the best one I had ever met. I had not ever considered loving anyone else. I could change for Justin. He was worth it. Who else would love me like he did? I cried and cried and cried until I was exhausted. I didn't want to talk with my sisters about this just yet so I just suffered in silence. I finally cried myself to sleep.

After a long, practically sleepless night, I just sat in my room to think. I would replay what happened in my head over and over again. I had not heard from him all day. I was hoping he would call, but he didn't. Was it really over? Was he as unhappy as I was? I started to cry again. I pretended all day that everything was okay. When my mom commented that she was surprised that I had not seen Justin every day that I had been home, I just laughed it off and said that he was working. Now that it was dark and everyone was asleep, I didn't have to pretend anymore. After I tossed and turned and cried most of the night, I finally fell asleep around 4:30 that morning. Maxine woke me up at 10:00. She admitted that she had heard me crying most of the night. She told me to spill it. I couldn't lie and say nothing was wrong, so I told her. Maxine is the middle girl. She is strong and has a good head on her shoulders and I trusted what Maxine thought even if she was younger than me. After I finished telling her what happened, she looked at me crazy and asked me if I had lost my mind. She told me that if I settled now that I would be settling for the rest of my life. If he loved me as much as I loved him, neither would have to give up their dream. She pointed out that relationships are about compromise and sacrifice, and that it's not just one sided. "Did he break up with you?" Maxine asked. "Yes, I think so." "Good." She responded. "Why would you say that?" "I see him talking to Michelle a little too much." My face started to feel hot. "Oh, that's why he isn't 'in love' with me anymore. Here I am sitting here crying like a fool and he is probably with her grinning in her face and telling her how he finally got rid of me." The more I thought about it, the madder I got. How is it that he is going to act as though he was doing me a favor? Then it hit me; maybe he did do me a favor.

I spent the remainder of my Christmas break enjoying my family and hanging out with my friend Carmen. It was a struggle to enjoy the holidays because I had expected to be with Justin, but I put on the happiest face I could around my family but cried like a baby when I was with Carmen where it was safe. There were times when I didn't know if I was crying because I was mad or because I was hurt. Truth be told, in this situation, they are probably one in the same. Hurt and anger go together like peanut butter and jelly. You just can't have one without the other. Carmen didn't pass judgment or tell me what she thought I should do. She just listened and made me laugh as much as she could. She even offered to go to Justin's house and hit him on the nose hard enough to knock him on his butt. Now that made me laugh! I knew she would do it too. That's what best friends are for.

I went back to Columbia in January with a broken heart. I was sad to leave the family, but I was happy to get away from Justin. I wasn't so sure that if I saw Justin again that I would remember that he had done me a favor by breaking up with me or run up and knock him on his butt.

Since I needed another elective for the spring semester because I'd failed my anatomy class in the fall, I took a Marriage and Family Therapy course. I was hooked. I changed my major from nursing to Marriage and Family Therapy. I finally figured out what I wanted to do with my life. I also took Speech Communications. Everyone had to take this course no matter your major. This is the class where I met Lorna Whyte. Lorna had failed an introductory accounting class and since this was a required elective she figured she would go ahead and take it and get it out of the way. We became instant friends, and have been friends ever since.

Lorna was also a freshman. She was in college working toward a business degree. She wanted to eventually earn her Master's in Business Administration. She was smart, so I know you are wondering why she failed her accounting class. Like me, she failed because she was in love. She also dated her high school sweetheart. She was able to go home on the weekends or he was able to come to visit her at Columbia the weekends that she didn't come home. He was quite a bit older than Lorna. She was eighteen like me, but he was twenty-one. A real man! I mean legal and everything, but he was too old for her. He was very possessive and wanted her to spend every minute she could with him on the weekends. When they weren't together, they were always on the telephone. No wonder she failed, she didn't have time to do anything but entertain him. When she failed her accounting class, she was placed on academic probation. She didn't fail her other three courses, but her grades were barely passing. A failed course, two C's and a D, meant her grade point average was below 2.0. If she didn't do better in the spring, she would be on academic suspension. Her parents were furious and told her that she could no longer come home as often on the weekends. She needed to study more and spend less time with what's his name. They knew his name was Patrick, but since they didn't like him, that is how they often referred to him. She hated it when they referred to him as "what's his name". They believed he was too old for her, but she just had to have him. It was 12:00 noon on Friday and Patrick had come to visit Lorna as usual. When she told her "man" that she wouldn't be able to come home as often as she did and that he couldn't visit her as much as he had been visiting because her grades had suffered, he simply looked at her and said, "That's what happens when you date young girls. Good luck with your future." He simply went back to his car and drove away. Lorna stood there stunned. She thought to herself "I know he didn't just drop me like a broken egg in an egg tossing contest. What am I supposed to do now?" For a brief moment, she thought that she didn't have anything to live for. Her grades had suffered, the man that she loved had just dumped her, and she didn't have any friends because she had spent so much time with what's his name. Now what was she to do?

The break up happened at her dorm outside in the quad where students often gathered to socialize. She hoped no one saw or heard what happened. She just turned and walked back to her dorm. Sat down and was about to cry when she saw his picture. She reached for it but knocked it over and broke the frame. She picked up the picture, frame, and the glass very carefully so she wouldn't cut her finger. She then noticed the back of the photo. The picture had originally belonged to Lisa. Who is Lisa? She started to get mad and then she remembered Dexter. Dexter was the boy she had dated from the age of fifteen to eighteen. She thought Dexter hung the moon until what's his name decided he was interested in her. Why would she date a boy when she could date a man? It dawned on her, she had dumped Dexter just as callously as what's his name had dumped her. What goes around comes back around. "Wow! Now I know how Dexter felt." Lorna was some kind of depressed, but knew she couldn't stay there long. She would have the weekend, alone, to think about what happened. The spring semester started on Monday. She needed an elective so she searched the student spring course offerings and saw Speech and Communications. She chuckled and said "Why not? I might as well get it over with." She arrived at the registrar's office just as it was closing for the weekend and added this class to her schedule.

The professor stated that we would have a group presentation due by the end of the course and that we needed to create a group, no more than four per group or no fewer than two. Groups formed quickly. Lorna and I were the odd ducks out, so we introduced ourselves and agreed to be partners. We talked about what we would present for our assignment. Lorna stated that we should do something about why relationships don't work. She said that she should know what it takes since she had just experienced a break up. I told her that I had experienced a break up over Christmas break. Since she had just gone through a break up and I had just gone through a break up, we hit it off. She became a fast and trusted friend. After all, I have been told misery loves company, even though this is not exactly the same thing. LOL! Whatever!

Since my relationship with Justin ended I was hard on all the guys who tried to date me. I didn't entertain any foolishness. If I thought a man was trying to play me, he was dismissed. I was done with compromising. Look what it got me. I was content being by myself if that meant I had to sacrifice so much of myself just to be with a man. I was licking my wounds and wanted to make sure that they would not be reopened for some clown just wanting to have a good time.

After I graduated from college with my undergraduate degree, I immediately began working on my graduate degree. I was so focused on earning my PhD that I didn't have time to do anything else, to include dating. Once I was finished earning all of my degrees, I needed to decide where I wanted to live. Lorna had headed back home to Seattle, Washington. She had finished her Master's degree in Business Administration, so she went home to find a job. I had visited her before on several occasions since she left, and thought it would be a great place to live. I thought about moving home, but I knew I would run into Justin, his wife Michelle, and their baby- the perfect little family. I just couldn't deal with that. It had been almost twelve years since our break-up. I knew that I was over him, but it was still going to be hard to see that he was making his dreams come true and mine appeared to be on hold. I had managed to avoid them when I went home to visit my family, but there was no way I could avoid them forever if we lived in the same city. I decided I would move to Seattle after I finished my doctoral degree, but before I could move, I would have to start looking for employment. Lorna told me about The Loving Hearts Counseling

Center, a non-profit agency that she thought would be perfect for me. She was right. After graduation, I moved to Seattle and was lucky to start working there immediately.

I thoroughly enjoyed working at Loving Hearts. While I was working on my marriage and family therapy degree, I had the opportunity to counsel patients. The focus of the therapy I was learning involved the entire family, but I have always had a soft spot for the woman in the family who was trying desperately to keep her family together. Loving Hearts allowed me to do that. Now that I had a dream job, I wanted more. I wanted someone to share it with. Maybe that's why when I met Preston, I stopped being so hard and decided to give him a chance. Not only did this man want to love and protect me; he was also supportive of my dreams. Let's keep it real; I also needed the loving that only a good man could give me. I was tired of being alone. I had met the requirements that my mom and dad insisted upon and that was my being able to take care of myself. When I met Preston, I knew that even though there was a chance of me getting hurt, I was willing to let him into my life and into my world. I wasn't going to miss out on this good thing because of past hurts. My hurts were where they needed to be, in the past. I allowed my defenses to come down and let him into my heart. For once, I decided to just go with my gut and allow my heart to follow. It hadn't led me wrong so far, and I prayed this wouldn't be the first time, but I was finally willing to risk it.

Chapter 3

Preston is a thirty-two year old man, who was a partner in a prestigious law firm in Seattle before he decided to branch out on his own. He had money from his dad's and grandparent's insurance policies, but he still worked to help put himself through college. He knew his grandparents would have been proud of the man that he had become. He wished that they were here to see how happy he was and to meet MacKenzie, the woman he had fallen in love with.

When Preston was ten, he was living in Orlando, Florida, with his parents. He enjoyed living in Orlando. It was the home of Walt Disney World. To him as a young boy, it was the best place to live on earth unless you were stuck in traffic with the tourists who had no idea where they were going. Either way, it was still the best place to live. Preston had aspired to work at Walt Disney World. His dream job was to be Mickey Mouse. He knew that there was a person inside of the costume and that he was not the real Mickey Mouse. He didn't care. All he could think of was how cool that would be to be the most loved character in the world.

He lived with his dad and his mom. He had no siblings. They were not rich. His dad worked in construction. His mom was a middle school teacher. Florida was notorious for summer storms. It felt like hurricanes were always on the radar. They had to make sure that during hurricane season, they had emergency supplies and were ready to evacuate at a moment's notice.

Preston had never experienced a hurricane and hoped he never would. All of that was about to change.

One September day, Preston was at school when the school was notified that a tropical storm was forming miles out into the ocean, but there was no need for alarm. The storm had not quite been identified as a tropical storm, but it looked as if it were headed that way. Orlando residents listened to the news intently for the next three days hoping the storm would head back out to sea. Unfortunately, it was heading towards land. Orlando residents were instructed to take precautions to ensure that they were prepared. Whenever this occurred people would go to the grocery stores and buy up all the canned goods, bread, peanut butter, jelly, and bottled water. Preston's parents would be right in there with them. It was a mad house because everyone always waited until the last minute, hoping the storm would turn. The storm often didn't, but every now and then it would.

The storm was now Tropical Storm Chris. When it came ashore, it came ashore with high wind gusts. They were howling winds at about sixty-five miles per hour. It was loud and scary. These were the times when Preston wished he had a sister or brother that he could be afraid with. Mom and Dad had each other, but he had no one. He didn't like being by himself. All of a sudden he heard a loud noise, a scream, and then nothing. It didn't sound like anything fell in or on the house, so he wondered why his mom screamed. Then there was complete silence. He was too afraid to move. His parents had always told him that he should stay put until one of them came to get him. Ordinarily he would have been in the room with his parents, but they didn't think the storm was bad enough to warrant them to all gather in one place for safety. They had expected lots of rain, high winds, and power outages, but nothing too serious so he lay in bed for hours until the storm had finally passed. At some point he must have fallen asleep because the next thing he remembered was hearing his dad's voice. He tried to hear what he was saying, but he couldn't quite make it out. He climbed out of his bed and was about to go to his parents' bedroom when his dad came in. His dad was visibly upset. Preston wondered what had happened that made his dad this upset. He had never seen his dad like this before. He was struggling not to cry. This frightened Preston. What he heard next frightened him even more. "Preston, during the storm last night when the lights went out, your mom tripped and fell and hit her head on the table beside our bed. She is hurt very badly. The paramedics were finally able to come and get her this morning. They took her to the hospital. I don't know how long she will be in the hospital, but I need to go and be with her. I called your grandparents to come and take care of you. They are trying to get a flight to Orlando today. Get dressed so that we can go to the hospital to check on your mother." Preston did as he was told without saying a word. He was worried about his mom and prayed that she would be okay.

When they arrived at the hospital, the nurse that was in the room with mom stated that they could only stay for a few minutes. She exited the room. His mom's head was bandaged and her eyes were closed. There were lots of tubes and machines. He didn't know what they were, but it was all very scary. The room smelled funny. He couldn't describe what he smelled; it was so different from anything he ever smelled before. He was very nervous and afraid to move. His dad said it was okay to talk to his mom, but he had to speak softly and that she would not be able to answer, but he was sure she would be able to hear him. Preston walked over to the side of her bed. He whispered as gently as he could, "I love you momma. I hope you come home soon." He wasn't sure that she had heard him until he thought he saw a slight smile on her face and a tear roll from her eye down the side of her face. He touched her hand. He squeezed it ever so gently trying to be careful that he didn't hurt her. She was able to move one of her fingers. Preston was so excited. She knew he was there. Then the nurse then came in and said that they had to leave so that she could rest. Preston's dad leaned over and kissed her face and whispered something in her ear that Preston couldn't hear and then they went home. His dad didn't say much. When he they got home, his dad just sat and stared for the most part. He went through the motions of feeding and taking care of Preston, but that was all he did.

Grandpa Fred and Grandma Edda were scheduled to arrive the next day around lunchtime. They were his mom's parents. Preston loved them very much. He was excited that they were coming because he knew that they would make sure everything was okay. They usually did. After Larry picked them up from the airport, they went straight to the hospital. Preston went with them. This visit was different. Preston could hear the doctor talking to his dad and grandparents saying too much blood. The injury was too great. He wondered what all of that meant.

Preston's mom was buried three days later. His mom died as result of a traumatic brain injury. She was only thirty-five years old. She was so beautiful. She was laying there in a pink casket, her favorite color, as if she were asleep. Preston understood that she wasn't. He knew that this would be the last time that he would see his mom. The next time he would see her would be in heaven. There were many people at the funeral. So many nice things were said about her. There were plants and flowers every-where. Many people said how much they liked and even loved her. This made Preston feel good, but nothing could take away his sadness and pain.

After the service was over, Preston went to his room to change his clothes. He went to the drawer that usually held the clothes that he changed into when he got home from school, but it was empty. He opened more drawers, but they were empty too. He went to his closet, nothing. What was going on? Just as he turned to go and ask his dad about his clothes, his dad walked in the room and sat on Preston's bed. "Where are my clothes dad?" "They are packed with all of your other things. You are going to live with grandpa and grandma in Seattle. I can't take care of you the way that I need to right now. Not the way that you deserve to be taken care of, so they have offered to allow you to come and live with them. I guess we are lucky you didn't have any brothers or sisters. Due to their age and lack of money, they can only take one person and that's you." He tried to make Preston feel special. "I know you are going to miss your mom and being here at home with me and your friends, but I can't care for you right now. I love you Preston. Never forget that. Do you understand?" For the first time since the funeral, he saw his dad cry. They held each other tightly. Preston cried too. He tried to understand why he had to leave, but he wasn't sure he did. He went with his grandparents to live in Seattle as he was told to do. That would be the last time he saw his dad alive.

Preston went to live with his grandparents in a town outside of Seattle called Victoria. It was beautiful. He remembered visiting their home once with his mom. He was happy that his grandparents loved him enough to take care of him until his dad could take care of him again, but he missed his mom so much, and all he wanted to do was go home and be with his dad. He felt empty and believed that he would feel that way forever. His grandparents' house had lots of trees that he could climb and be alone with his thoughts. He tried to be brave because he thought that was what his dad and grandparents would want him to do. He allowed himself to cry one last time high up in the trees where he thought no one could see him but God, and then he was done. He still experienced the sadness of losing his mom and missing his dad, but he tried to concentrate on the happy times they had together. That's what kept him going.

He remained with his grandparents throughout middle and high school. He was now eighteen and graduating from high school. He had spoken with his dad several times about coming to his graduation. He stated that he would be there no matter what. Preston was so excited. He had not seen his dad since that day when he left Orlando at the age of ten. His dad had called often and tried many times to come out to see him in Seattle, but he was never able to come. He wouldn't allow Preston to come home to Orlando to see him no matter how much he begged. Whenever Preston would bring up the subject of coming back to Orlando or his dad coming to Victoria, his dad would change the subject or simply say that he would see him soon. That time never came.

Preston's Grandma Edda was very sweet and loving. He knew his mom must have gotten her sweetness and loving ways from her. She often hugged and kissed him reassuring him that everything was going to be okay. When he would start to miss his mom she would pull out pictures of her and tell him stories of when she was young. He was a lot like her.

His grandparents did not have much money, but Preston had everything he needed. Grandpa often took him fishing and tried to guide him as much as he could through his teen years. Grandpa told him stories about his youth and how he always wanted to be a lawyer. He never had the opportunity to become a lawyer because he had to work and help take care of his younger brothers and sisters after his dad died. He stated that he had always wanted his own business, but family came first. Preston was so proud of his grandpa and wanted to be like him.

Preston's dad was supposed to be flying into Seattle for his high school graduation, but never made it. He worried that something had happened because his dad didn't come and he had not called. He tried to enjoy the ceremony, but his worry continued. "Why wasn't he there?" After the commencement exercises were over and Preston was at home changing to go out to celebrate with his friends, the telephone rang. Grandma Edda answered the telephone. It was a doctor from a Florida hospital. He was sorry to report that his dad had died early that afternoon. The immediate cause of death was not provided to Grandma Edda because an autopsy had to be performed. When Preston received the news about his dad's death, he was devastated. He didn't know if he should be angry or sad. His emotions were all over the place. He felt like he was about to scream, Grandma Edda touched his hand ever so gently. He turned to face her and collapsed into her embrace. She always made everything all right. Grandpa Frank and Grandpa Edda would take Preston back to Orlando to bury his dad.

When they reached Orlando, they took a taxi to the county hospital's morgue to claim his dad's body so that he could be laid to rest. Preston was glad that his grandparents were there because he had no idea what to do or what to expect. They identified Larry and took his belongings. Since they had arrived early on a Monday morning, they had time to contact the funeral home that handled his mother's funeral to come and pick up Larry's body. After that was settled, a shocked and overwhelmed Preston wanted to go to the house where he had lived with his mom and dad. He thought this would help him find the peace he desperately needed. A place where there were happy memories before his life unraveled. His grandparents stated that they needed to get a rental car so that they would be able to take care of things and not spend much money on taxis. They returned to the airport, rented a car, and headed to the house.

When they arrived at the house, it didn't look the same. There were no cars in the driveway so they parked. Grandpa Frank took out Larry's keys from his things and tried to unlock the door to the house. By this time a car drove up. A man got out of the car and approached them. He seemed very angry. "Who are you and what do you think you are doing? You trying to break into my house old man?" Grandpa Frank was startled by the man's reaction and question. "No, I was trying to get into the home of my son-in-law who died a few days ago." "Well, this ain't it. I have been living here for the last three years. I am sorry for your loss, but you should be careful." Grandpa apologized for our trespassing, after speaking with the man for a few minutes, he walked back to the car where grandma and I were waiting. We all sat there shocked. What could this man be talking about? This was his family's house. Grandpa pulled out Larry's wallet that held his driver's license. The address listed on the license was an apartment. Grandpa stopped by a gas station to ask for directions. The apartment was about fifteen minutes from the house where they once lived. The apartment was barely furnished and it didn't look like anything that Preston had ever experienced. His confusion continued to grow. He had never remembered living this way. His mom had always made sure their house was clean and in order. What could have happened?

The memorial service was held on Wednesday. Grandpa and grandma had arranged for Larry to be laid to rest beside his wife. They paid what they could so the service would have to be small. They asked that the death certificate be forwarded to them once it was prepared. They agreed to their request. He was forty-five years old.

There were many people who came to the service. They shared their condolences and shared how much they liked Larry and Alice, his parents and how proud they were of Preston graduating from high school. As soon as the service was over, they went back to Larry's apartment to sort through his things. Preston was encouraged to take anything he wanted to help him remember his dad. While Preston was rummaging through his dad's things, his grandparents went through mounds of paperwork.

They found an insurance policy that Larry had on himself. They took it and would contact the insurance company later. Grandma Edda found a letter addressed to Preston from his dad. She showed it to Grandpa Frank. They decided not to show it to him right away because they knew that whatever was written in the letter was going to upset him even more than he already was. Since he was already having a hard time dealing with his dad's death, they decided to place among the papers that they were taking back to Victoria and that they would give it to him when they felt the time was right.

They were boxing up all the items that would be donated to the Salvation Army, when there was a knock at the door. It was one of Larry's friends who had attended the funeral. He stated that he was checking on Preston because he knew that everything that he had heard would be upsetting. Preston and his grandparents were confused. The gentleman shared that Larry had been so grief stricken when Alice died, that he never stopped mourning her. He was injured on the job and couldn't work so he eventually lost his job and then the house. He shared that all Larry ever talked about was how proud he was of Preston and all he wanted to do was to see him, but he couldn't afford to go out to Seattle and see him nor send for him. Preston couldn't hear anymore. He walked outside to gather himself. What happened? Preston was always so sure that he knew what was going on with his dad, now he knew that things were not as they seemed. He wanted to ask his grandparents, but he knew this was not the time. He would hold his questions until later. It was time to go. Preston's life in Orlando was officially over.

Once Preston and his grandparents returned to Seattle they tried to make things as normal as possible, but they knew it would take time because Preston was trying to heal from his hurt and disappointment. His mother grew up in the church and she made sure that Preston went as well. She wanted him to have a relationship with the Lord. This was very important to him now that he had lost his mom and dad. He prayed for the Lord to help him. He felt so broken.

He continued to go to church with his grandparents. It was a source of strength for him that he needed now more than ever. He was devastated and angry that his dad wouldn't allow him to be with him after his mom died. After all he had lost her too. Preston was just left with feelings of anger, emptiness, abandonment, and confusion. What was he supposed to do with these emotions? Here he was a high school graduate and the thing that he wanted the most, he would be denied, and that was to see his dad again. He wanted to be sure that his dad was proud that he was graduating from high school. He knew his dad was proud because he told him often that he was proud that he was his son. When Preston mentioned that he wanted to be an attorney, his dad had encouraged him to be an attorney or whatever he wanted to be in life because he would be proud of him no matter what. He told him that he would help him as much as he could. He did help Preston, but not in the way he thought or imagined.

Grandpa Frank pulled out the insurance policy that he had taken from the house. Preston's dad had left him an insurance policy worth $50,000. This would be more than enough for Preston to begin college. The last thing Grandpa Frank did was encourage Preston to go to college to be an attorney. He promised him that he would. His grandparents had been married for 60 years when his grandpa had a heart attack and died at the age of 85. He died exactly one month after his dad had died.

In the fall, Preston was accepted to the University of Washington, in Seattle. His grandmother was so proud. Preston was all she had and Grandma Edda was all he had. He wanted to live at home and take care of her. She had celebrated her 80th birthday and he wanted to be with her as much as possible to help her out around the house, but there was a two-hour ride one way to and from school. Grandma Edda told him that he needed that time to study and he needed to stay on campus throughout the week and that she would be okay until he came home on the weekend. Grandma Edda finally convinced him to live in the dorm. Getting into college was easy, but getting into a good law school would be tough and it would be even tougher to stay in, yet he was determined that he would do it for his mom, dad, grandpa, and his grandma. Most of all, he would do it for himself.

After two years of college, Preston had to say his goodbyes to Grandma Edda. She was the last of the life that he knew. He was now a 20 year old man and feeling like that ten year old boy back in Orlando who had just lost his mom. Just when he thought things were getting back to normal, he had to deal with loss all over again. He just thought to himself that he knew that he had not fully gotten over losing his dad and grandpa, and now his sweet Grandma Edda was gone. What was he supposed to do now? He had nobody. Once again, he felt alone, lost, and wondered who would love him now. After she passed, Preston would visit the house often to make sure that everything was in order. Grandma had left him the house and all of her and his grandfather's worldly possessions. He would gladly give it up if he could have her back. She was his rock and without her he felt as if he no longer had roots or belonged anywhere except her house. His college tuition was paid for thanks to the insurance policy his dad had left to him. He had a house to live in once he graduated, if he so desired to live there, but it seemed so big and empty without her. He just couldn't imagine living there without his grandparents, especially Grandma Edda, but he knew the money wouldn't last forever and at least he knew he had somewhere to live. Preston knew for sure that the thing that he truly needed in life couldn't be purchased. For once, he was happy that he was an only child. Even though he was lonely sometimes as a child, he never had to share his parents or grandparents with anyone. If he were lucky enough to find love like his parents and grandparents had, he would only have one child so that he/she wouldn't have to divide his love among his children. He knew it sounded selfish, but that's how he felt. He'd hoped the woman he would marry would be okay with his reasoning.

While he was sitting in the family room lost in thought, he decided to get up and go into his grandparents' room. While he stood there looking around the room he saw the box they brought back from Orlando with a lot of papers that belonged to his dad. He went through it carefully. He thought most of it was junk, but he found information about his dad's old construction company. It had a lot of legal terminology that was easy to understand, but had a few items that he would need help with. He read something about a lawsuit that his dad had filed against them for an injury that he sustained on the worksite. Preston continued to dig, but didn't find anything else about what appeared to be a pending law suit against the construction company. Preston found the letter addressed to him. It was from his dad. He opened it with excitement. He was also nervous since he knew these would be the final words that he would hear directly from his dad.

Dear Preston,

I am so proud of you son. When you receive this letter, I will have missed your high school graduation and for that I am truly sorry. I need you to know that I wanted to tell you something so many times, but didn't have the courage. Where do I begin? It was my fault that your mom died. She and I were having an argument and she was trying to walk away from me when I grabbed her arm. She snatched away from me, fell, and hit her head on the nightstand next to our bed. I didn't call the ambulance right away because I was scared they would blame me for her accident. I am so sorry son. After you left, the police did an investigation and I was sentenced to three years for voluntary manslaughter. Even though I didn't mean to hurt her, because I didn't call the ambulance right away and she died, I was charged with a crime. I went to prison when you were eleven and I was released when you were fourteen. We were able to talk while I was in prison because your grandparents allowed me to call collect so that you wouldn't know where I was. While I was in the prison, I had time to pray and ask the Lord for forgiveness. I know that He did, but I couldn't forgive myself. A huge part of me died when your mom died. The other part died when I couldn't be with you. I couldn't bear the thought of you knowing what really happened, but I couldn't leave this world without telling you and asking for your forgiveness. Your grandparents forgave me, but I knew that our relationship would be forever damaged. They agreed to accept collect calls from me so that we could continue our relationship. I know it was difficult for them, but they did it for you. In my papers you will find information where I was filing a suit against the construction company for an injury I sustained on the job. I think I have left you enough information for you to go forward with my case. I am sorry I couldn't do more for you, but after being released from prison, I had nothing. Before I went to prison, I had lost everything because I couldn't work. The man who owns the apartment building where I live provides housing to ex-cons. He allowed me to do odd jobs around the complex so that I could continue living there at little to no cost. The money I had in the bank before I went to prison was still there, so I was able to eat and keep the lights on in the apartment. I was so embarrassed to be living that way that I never wanted you to see me like this. Please know how sorry I am and that I loved you and your mother with all my heart. I love you son. Dad

By the time Preston read the final words of the letter, he was standing in the middle of the room and shaking. His head was pounding so loudly that he could hear his heart beating in his ears. He was grinding his teeth and trying to steady himself because the room was spinning. He felt completely out of control. He felt like screaming…so he did. Preston screamed and screamed and screamed until he fell on the floor drenched in his own sweat. It took him a minute to realize that this was not some awful joke. This was real. He felt anger. He felt anger for a long time. He didn't know how long this anger would last, but he was there and that's all he knew.

News traveled fast in Victoria. When women heard about his perceived wealth, they decided that he needed someone to spend it on. He had the $50,000 to pay for school, so he didn't know why they thought he was rich, and he really didn't care. He was numb. He never knew if women were with him for him or for what they thought he had. He knew they were going to be disappointed when they figured out that he didn't really have any money. Oh well, he was going to make the rumors work for him. Little did they know that the money that wasn't being used for college was being saved. He still had plans of attending law school, so he had to spend wisely and he needed to find a job. He wanted to someday own his own law firm. He allowed them to think what they liked. He pretended to be a baller for a while, but soon found that it got old fast. The anger that he felt had started to subside. If he was going to find a woman like his dad and grandpa had found, he was definitely going about it the wrong way.

Preston worked hard to finish his undergraduate degree in Political Science. While he was working on his undergraduate degree during his fourth year of college, he landed an internship at a local law firm. They were very impressed with him. He was a hard worker, he learned very quickly, and most of all he was free. Preston didn't care about working for free right now. He was trying to get his foot in the door and he was doing an amazing job. This firm specialized in corporate law, but he figured they would have the right connections to someone who could help him with the letter that he found concerning the construction company and his dad's injury.

After Preston graduated, he was accepted into law school. That was the best news he had received in a long time. He was happy to be kept busy. It kept his mind from wondering back to his dad's letter. Every time he thought about it he would get angry all over again. To cope with his anger; he started drinking heavily. The alcohol dulled his pain and allowed him to forget everything. He was so happy when he found out he was accepted to law school that he decided to party with some friends. He drank so much he was sick for days. When he couldn't shake his symptoms of falling asleep and losing track of time, vomiting, and falling over things, he finally went to the hospital. When he was examined, he was told that he had a mild case of alcohol poisoning and that he was lucky because it could have been worse. He was admitted for treatment. As he lay in the bed, he reflected on his life and what it had become. He was cold and callous with enough anger that if anger were food, he could feed a third world country. He realized at that point that he was so consumed with anger that he would be unable to move forward and find happiness. He was on a self-destructive path that needed to change before he lost everything. He decided that he couldn't change the past and that all he could do was move forward. That meant that he was going to have to forgive his dad and release the anger that had been controlling him for the last year. Preston closed his eyes, whispered the Lord's Prayer, and said, "Lord, I forgive him." He fell asleep. He remained in the hospital overnight. When he went home, he emptied every bottle of Jack Daniels he could find. He kissed each one of them goodbye and he was done.

Preston was lucky that he was on a break from school and

his internship when all of this happened. He realized he could have lost his future trying to hold on to the past. He thought that what he done to himself would hurt his grandparents and mom. Preston then realized he had no idea how he got home that night. After lying around for a few days, he decided to re-join the living. He went to a local restaurant. He had not gone grocery shopping in a while so he had no choice, but to eat out. He sat at the bar and was about to order a cheeseburger and fries when Jamal walked up. He said, "Hey man, you alright?" Preston looked at him puzzled and asked, "Do I know you?" Jamal burst into laughter. "I didn't figure you would remember me. You were pretty toasted at the Pritty Kitty Club a week ago." "The Pritty Kitty?" "Yes, you were so drunk the owner wouldn't allow you to drive home, so he had me and one of my boys drive you home.""How did you know where I lived?" "Driver's license, dude." They both burst into laughter. " "Preciate it man. You probably saved my life. Hey, let me hook you up with a burger." "Cool." After a few minutes of talking about school and sports, Jamal asked Preston where he went to church. "I used to go to church with my grandparents before they died, but I haven't been there in about a year. It's hard to go there and not expect to see them." "Man, I'm sorry to hear that. I attend The Holiness of God Church of the Living Word. Why don't you come and visit?" "O, okay. I will think about it." But Preston knew he wasn't ready to go to another church. When he was going to church, he was still attending the church his grandparents went to every Sunday before they passed away. For right now that was his church even if he couldn't bring himself to go. After sharing a meal and root beer, they separated agreeing to hang out again soon. Turns out Jamal also attended the University of Washington and had seen Preston around campus and had intended to become friends with him sooner. He figured this tall good-looking brother could pull the women and he could have the rejects. Don't get me wrong, Jamal is extremely good looking, but a man standing 5'4" tall doesn't get a lot of play. Jamal felt as if all the women of the Amazon jungle were attending the University of Washington and he needed a strategy to land one of them. A man has to have a plan.

When Preston started classes and returned to the firm to complete a second internship, he was pleasantly surprised that they were going to pay him a stipend and offer to pay a portion of his tuition if he agreed to work for the firm for five years after he completed his law degree. Cha-ching! He had hit the jackpot. Preston played it cool when he accepted their offer. After all, this was the best firm in the area and there was no way he was going to pass this up. Things were finally looking up for Preston. He excused himself saying he had to go the restroom. He went into the restroom. He checked under the stalls to make sure he was alone and he jumped around and screamed "Thank You Jesus!" just above a whisper. After he celebrated for what felt like forever, but was actually only about one minute, he went back to his assigned workspace like nothing happened. Once he was off, he called Jamal to tell him the good news. He and Jamal had been hanging out quite a bit and Preston enjoyed having a true friend.

Jamal suggested that they go out and celebrate. Since it was a Tuesday afternoon when Preston got the news, they had to wait until the weekend before they could hang out. Jamal suggested that they go to the Pritty Kitty. Preston was down with that. They arrived around 10:00 Friday night. Jamal introduced Preston to the owner who was his uncle. Jamal and Preston were acting as if they were VIPs and that was attracting the women. Initially Preston loved the attention, but realized he needed more out his life. He was twenty-four years old and just starting law school. He needed to keep his own head on straight. Don't get me wrong, he smiled and flirted and danced up on a few women, but when they started asking too many questions, and made it known that they always wanted an attorney for a husband. They might as well have been Charlie Brown's teacher. All he heard was wonk, wonk, wonk, wonk, wonk. Each time he experienced the same thing. Preston wasn't stupid so he knew what he needed to do. He enjoyed looking at scarcely dressed women with the best of them, but it wasn't what he was about, at least not tonight. He was definitely going to give it a try again real soon. LOL!

Preston continued to work hard in school and at the firm. To make his dream of having his own law firm he would need to make excellent contacts and create a name for himself that is synonymous with integrity and outstanding results. After five years, and a well-established client base, he decided to branch out on his own. With the faith of God, he opened his own law firm at the age of thirty. He had money, his law firm, yet there was still something missing.

After two years of establishing his law firm into one of the top law firms in Seattle's metropolitan area, Preston finally decided to go to Jamal's church. Jamal said he thought he would enjoy the services and there were some fine women there so that made it even better. Preston just laughed and decided he would meet him there on Sunday. Sure enough Preston enjoyed the services and definitely enjoyed all the eye candy. There was one particular woman there who caught his eye and he wanted to meet her. You got it. It was MacKenzie. Preston was the one who asked Jamal to talk to MacKenzie and ask her about a restaurant in the area so he would have the opportunity to meet her. You know the rest.

He believed that it was fate when he met MacKenzie. She had that loving spirit that his mom and grandmother had. She wasn't materialistic and that pleased him even more. She was sweet, but could have a little fire and that excited him. He thought his parents and grandparents would have loved her as much as he did. He never knew his paternal grandparents, but thought they would have been proud as well. Preston would always get lost in his thoughts when he drove out to his grandparents' house. He decided he would stay out there overnight. It was always nice to be at their house. This is where he could feel all the love he needed.

Chapter 4

I suggested that we seek spiritual counseling before we got married. I don't know where that thought came from, but it came to my mind and out of my mouth it came. He agreed to it. Like he wasn't going to, right? We were in counseling once a week with pastor for six weeks. We learned so much about each other. So far, nothing I heard frightened me. And praise the Lord nothing I said frightened him. Well, it was confirmed. We were going to announce to the congregation that we were to be married on December 31st. At the stroke of midnight we would be Mr. Preston and Dr. MacKenzie Stone. We didn't have much time. I had to get things together in about six months. I had plenty of money saved so all I had to do was buy the dress I found the same day I met Preston (a girl had to claim him). My parents and sisters Maxine and Sandra would be flying in on Christmas Eve, and my girl Carmen would be flying in December 29th. Everything was perfect….except one thing; I still didn't know where Preston lived! I had asked several times, but he was always evasive. He should know by now that it wouldn't matter. He would always say it was a surprise. One day he asked if I trusted him and was willing to allow him to surprise me. I had always said yes. Bump that junk, I wanted to know! I needed to know!

My people arrived as scheduled on Christmas Eve. I was so excited. They couldn't wait to meet their future son-in-law and brother-in-law. I couldn't believe I was about to marry a man that my parents nor my sisters had met. What if they didn't like him? What if he had been dating one of them all along? My Lord, had my imagination taken off or what? This is what happens when you only rely on only what you can see and touch.

On December 29th, Carmen arrived. There is no way I would get married without her being there. Carmen is my girl from back home. We have been friends since we were ten. It was going to be so good to see her.

When I arrived at the airport her plane had already landed. Where is she? I walked the airport for about twenty minutes when I heard a voice say "Mickey!" I knew that it could only be my girl because no one else knows me by that name but my peeps. I turned around and there she was. She looked so good and I had missed her so much. Our weekly telephone calls were simply not like seeing my friend in person. We were so happy to be together again, when we embraced we just cried. After we all got settled in at my house, I shared the plans for the wedding and set up a time for them to meet my Preston. We were talking ninety to nothing. My mom and dad just laughed like they always did when the four of us were together. Now she had a new one to enjoy as well, my girl Lorna. Everyone got along instantly. I couldn't have been happier. We enjoyed spending those days together. I tried to solicit help in planning my wedding, but my parents and sisters kept distracting me. They weren't much help at all. It was really beginning to get on my nerves. My mom finally said, "MacKenzie, take care of your dress and we've got the rest." I couldn't believe how calm and nonchalant everyone was while I was only trying to plan my wedding. I started to protest, but I knew better. I was already stressed and I didn't want to have to deal with my mom so I let it go. I thought I heard them snickering when I walked off, but I knew I was stressed to the maximum, so I just went to my bedroom to gather my thoughts.

I was about to be married and it came to me again that I had not seen where Preston lived. I was determined that I was going to see this house. I would not be denied. I called Preston to let him know that the remainder of my family had arrived and that I was ready for him to meet them. He said he was ready when I was. He suggested that we meet the next day at a restaurant near the bay. I suggested that we meet somewhere more quaint, like his house. He laughed and said "MacKenzie, soon enough baby, soon enough." No he didn't! I agreed hesitantly and let it go…for now.

The following day as we were preparing to leave the house and head to the restaurant the doorbell rang. I looked at everyone as if saying "Who could that be?" They all laughed. Lorna said "Your house?" as if she was saying Duh? How would we know? I looked through the peephole. There was a short, but good looking man standing at the door. I thought he looked familiar but I wasn't sure where I had seen this man before. I opened the door and then it dawned on me, it was Jamal. "Jamal, what are you doing here?" I introduced him to everyone and asked again, "What are you doing here?" He responded, "I heard that there were some fine women and a distinguished gentleman here that were supposed to be meeting a friend of mine and he thought you may need a ride." We looked out and saw a stretch white limousine. We screamed and ran for the limo. We lost all of our cool points. As we were riding, I looked around and determined that we were nowhere near where we were supposed to be going. I tapped on the window, "Jamal where are we going?" He just smiled and stated that it was a surprise. Lorna had a look on her face that I had only seen when she was up to something. I gave her that side look and she just shook her head and asked, "Why are you looking at me?" They all looked at each other and giggled. Maxine told me to chill because she had a good feeling about this.

We traveled about another ten minutes when we pulled up to

this beautiful mansion. Jamal used the telephone in the limousine and the gate opened. We all looked in disbelief at what we saw. It was a large brick house, with a long winding driveway. It had a well-manicured lawn. Beautiful tulip beds and many other blooming flowers all around that made it appear as if it were a greeting card. I was lost in the majesty of what I could have only imagined Heaven was like. Even in the dark, you knew that this was the most beautiful place that you could ever have imagined. When the car stopped, Jamal jumped out and opened the door and let us out. We giggled and couldn't contain ourselves any longer. We laughed and carried on something awful. We just couldn't contain our excitement not a moment longer. We were led into a foyer with elegant marble floors and then into the most beautiful red colored dining room. The high back chairs were hand crafted. They looked so good we were afraid to sit on them. We were seated by a very nice elderly woman, who was just beaming with the sweetest smile I had ever seen. She said "Come on in babies. We've been expecting you. Please have a seat." As I started to introduce myself, she interrupted saying "I know who you are baby." I guess that this sweet exquisite lady here is your mother." I said yes, and introduced the rest of our entourage. Of course when she commented on how handsome my dad was, his chest blew up so big I thought he had stopped breathing. I was feeling like I was someone special and on top of the world. We were seated and having tea when Preston walked in. He was looking more beautiful than I had ever seen him. He was wearing a black tux that made me bite my lip. He looked so good. You could see every tooth in that room. Everyone was grinning so hard you would think that we were doing a toothpaste commercial. After I finished the introductions, we all were invited into another room to relax before dinner was served. I thought we were in the dining room. You can tell when people aren't use to anything. Preston motioned for me to remain for a few minutes. He wanted to speak with me privately. Everyone else moved ahead of me. After everyone went in he turned and smiled so sweetly and asked me "MacKenzie will you marry me?" I looked at him and smiled and said, "I believe I already said yes." He said "No, I mean now?" "Right now?" "Yes" he said. "Right now!" My mouth dropped open and I was speechless. My mom stuck her head through the door and said "Girl are you coming or what? We have got to get you dressed." I was so moved I could hardly keep it together. I looked into those brown eyes and said "Yes. Right now!" He kissed me sweetly on the cheek then my mom took me by the arm and she and the ladies rushed me off to get dressed.

My wedding dress, my make-up, you name it, it was there. How did they pull this off? I couldn't believe this! If it was a fairy tale, I didn't ever want to wake up! We all scrambled around trying to get me dressed as quickly as possible. I was so overjoyed that I couldn't contain myself. I looked at Lorna. "You are the only way this could have happened. How did you pull this off?" "Later, you have a fine man waiting for you. You have plenty of time to get the details later." We embraced as we fought back tears. "I am so blessed!"

When I entered the ballroom everyone was there. The pastor, my church family, I mean everyone! Lorna is good! I started to cry, I was so overwhelmed. The ceremony was beautiful. Everything I had planned, he and my people made it happen. I loved it! This was the most perfect wedding I could have ever imagined. Now to top it all off, this grand ball room in which we just shared our vows is a part of the biggest surprise of all. Preston turned and said "Surprise My Queen! You are home!" I felt like I was going to faint. This mansion was mine. This is mine! Preston explained that he had to be sure that I didn't know about his money before he showed me where he lived. "Money? How much money are we talking about?" Preston stated that he was worth more than I could spend, he hoped. LOL! He owned The Law Office of Preston Stone, PLLC. It was one of the top law firms in Seattle. My mild mannered Preston was one of the top corporate attorneys in the country and he was mine, all mine. "Thank you Jesus!" How in the world could he have this much money? He would later explain that he paid for college with the life insurance policy his dad left for him when he died. He also shared that there was a lawsuit pending against the construction company for an injury his dad sustained while on the job. Not only was he injured; he was also fired when he couldn't return to work. They also neglected to pay his medical bills, which contributed to his death. By the time the attorney was done with them, Preston was awarded $400,000, to include back pay. Because he worked with corporate lawyers they knew investors who helped Preston invest his money. With his investments, the earnings from his position with the firm, and his law degree, he was able to establish an outstanding reputation so that he could branch out on his own and continue to be successful.

We were supposed to be married on New Year's Eve. During watch night services we were to celebrate the ending of a perfect year and start our new life as husband and wife. We were looking forward to the next year and what it had to hold…or so we thought. In order to pull off the surprise we had to get married on December 30th. We all attended church on December 31, for watch night services. At the stroke of midnight we left the church and headed to the airport to catch a redeye to our honeymoon destination. I didn't know where we were going and I didn't care as long as I was with my Preston. My family stayed at my new home until the Saturday after the New Year's Holiday and then they headed home.

I can't believe it. We are in Aspen. Do black people go to Aspen? Have I seen any black people since I've arrived in Aspen? Just as that thought was complete, I bumped into none other than Dr. Celeste Morgan. Yes, I guess black people go skiing too.

Chapter 5

Dr. Morgan is a successful black obstetrician/gynecologist. She is a petite young woman who only stands about four feet eleven inches tall. She is quite beautiful. I asked how she was and why she was in Aspen. She stated that she was there for an in vitro fertilization conference. I introduced her to Preston as we sipped our lattes, we exchanged small pleasantries and then we parted company. Preston and I checked into the honeymoon suite and the festivities began, if you know what I mean.

It was 9:00 a.m. as I sat and gazed out of the window, mesmerized by what I saw as Preston slept. He was sleeping so peacefully. My thoughts were filled with his face, his forehead, and his perfectly shaped brows that hovered above the most beautiful brown eyes I had ever seen. This was a feeling I hoped would never end. I was a woman in love, hopelessly and completely in love.

I made sure I was quiet as I moved about the room so that I could position myself in front of the window. I peered through the small opening in the curtains. Aspen was breathtakingly beautiful. Snow covered everything as far as the eye could see. There was no prediction of snow according to the weather forecast, but there it was flowing slowly and deliberately from the sky. It appeared to be falling like powdered sugar from a shifter onto a freshly baked angel food cake. The more it fell, the more the ground disappeared. The smell and sound of the logs in the fireplace made for a perfect start to the day.

The average temperature was about 30 degrees, but all I could think was I wanted to get out and experience the snow. I had never been to Aspen so I wanted to do everything and experience everything there was to Aspen. It was nice and toasty in the room, but I still had to wrap myself in a blanket to keep from getting a chill. The last thing I wanted to do was to get sick on my honeymoon.

I could see the ski lift from our window and all the people who headed up the slope to do some skiing. Wow! I imagined myself on the bunny slope learning to stand on the skis. I could see me crouched with my butt stuck up in the air as I leaned forward to gain my balance and……bam! I am on the ground. I giggled quietly to myself. I looked back at Preston to make sure I had not awakened him. He was still sleeping. I was hungry and ready to hit the slopes. I needed to wake him up. I went to the bed and leaned over him thinking that would stir him. No luck. How was I going to get this man up? If I get back in the bed with him and wake him up, I can forget about getting back out of it anytime soon. That's a tempting thought, smiling mischievously for a second. "Snap out of it girl, you are on a mission."

I have never been accused of being able to sing. If this doesn't get him up, nothing will. Preston laughs every time I sing. I know love gives you rose colored glasses, but it does nothing for the other persons hearing. Alright, what will I sing? Then it came to me. My sister use to sing Jennifer Holiday's, "And I Am Telling You I'm Not Goin," and it made our dog howl. Just thinking about it made me laugh out loudly. Well, it's now or never. I went into the bathroom and grabbed a complementary toothbrush from the counter. A big grin came over my face and I almost lost it I was giggling so hard. When I reached the doorway, I let it go to the top of my voice, "And I am telling you, I'm not goin'. You're the best man I've ever known, there's no way I could ever go"…Just as I was about to hit the No, No, No No way, Preston came up off the bed with a pillow in his hand. Yep, I think he's up! I squealed and started running. The chase was on. He chased me around the room as I continued to sing to the top of my voice, laughing hysterically. He was unsuccessful at catching me for the same reason. I jumped on the bed and belted out the verse about tearing down the mountains, yell, scream, and shout…and that's what I did when he grabbed my leg and yanked it from under me and I fell on the bed. Initially, he thought I was hurt because I had rolled onto my stomach and he couldn't see my face. I was laughing so hard that there was no sound. I was shaking. He wasn't sure what was happening. He grabbed me, "MacKenzie! MacKenzie!" At this point, he rolled me over and realized I was laughing. He busted out laughing. He was laughing so hard; he fell off the bed onto the floor. It took us another five minutes to recover from that event. Once he was able to pull himself together, he looked at me and asked ever so seriously, "Baby, are you going to get me up like this every morning while we are here?" I just smiled and said, "Maybe." We both burst into laughter again. I know he was thinking, "I am never letting her get up first again".

We started to get dressed. He turned and asked what I wanted to do. "After breakfast, I want to go the bunny slope and learn how to ski, or at least be able to stand up on the skis. " "Cool, let's do it. I wonder if they eat grits here in Colorado." I laughed out loudly and said, "There's only one way to find out."

Breakfast was filling, but no grits. Good thing we eat oatmeal. We rented skis, poles, and the whole nine so we could learn to ski. Preston went first. I had my phone out ready to take pictures of his falling, but it was so cold, my cell phone kept freezing. There was a photographer there who had the proper equipment to take pictures, so we asked him to take pictures of us trying to ski. Preston is very athletic so he did a great job of being able to stand on the skis and get to the bottom of the bunny slope before he fell. I made sure I got plenty of pictures of him on his bottom. Well, it was my turn. I did a great job of getting up on the skis. It was definitely harder than it looked. I kept thinking, if I can roller skate and roller blade, surely I should be able to do this. Well, I was correct in theory only. The snow is tricky. It was not a flat surface so all of that logical thinking went right up into the air and my feet did the same thing. Boom, I was on the ground. It was so much fun. We laughed and laughed and I got great pictures to remember our honeymoon. We were the only chocolate bunnies on the snow. That's cool; at least we won't lose one another.

We were outside for about two hours before we headed in. We went into the lobby to return our snow gear when we ran into Dr. Morgan again. She smiled at us and said, "Hey I saw you guys out on the snow. It looked like fun. ""Yes, it was. We will see just how much fun later on when I sit down." Preston started laughing. "Don't laugh Boo. You ate it a few times yourself." We all laughed. Dr. Morgan said, "It is so cold. Would you guys like some hot chocolate or coffee?" "That sounds like a plan. Hot chocolate please," I said. Preston stated that he could go for some hot chocolate as well. "Three hot chocolates coming up." We agreed to meet by the fire and off she went.

She was gone for only a few minutes. She returned with three large cups of hot chocolate. She handed Preston one first and then one to me. "Marshmallows!" I exclaimed. "Hey, I didn't get any marshmallows" exclaimed Preston. "Only for the ladies" I teased. We all laughed. After taking a couple of sips of her drink, Dr. Morgan then excused herself stating that she needed to get back to her conference. We said our goodbyes and she was gone.

The rest of the day was as wonderful as it started. We had lunch and went back to our room. We decided to get into the hot tub to warm up and sip cups of warm apple cider. I learned early in life that I had a low tolerance for alcohol, so I just don't bother. Preston used to drink in college, but decided it wasn't something he cared to do anymore. So cider was perfect for us. After an afternoon of shopping, a huge dinner, and an evening of enjoying each other's company, we settled in for the night. Preston had just placed more logs on the fire and snuggled in beside me when I felt a sharp pain on the right side of my stomach. At first I thought I had gas and that it would pass. No pun intended. I told Preston I thought I had gas so beware. We both laughed as he motioned as if he were going to get out of the bed.

The next couple of hours, the pain increased. I felt hot and thought I may have been running a fever. Preston had dozed off and I didn't want to wake him up, but I was starting to get concerned. All of sudden, the pain intensified to a point of making me groan so loudly that it woke Preston. He looked at me, touched my face, jumped out of the bed and ran to the bathroom. He came back with a thermometer and a cool cloth that he placed on my forehead. He took my temperature. It was 102. He asked how long I had been feeling bad; if I was nauseous; if I had pain. I said yes to all of the above. He called the front desk and asked for directions to the nearest hospital because I was sick. The concierge stated that the resort would transport me, but they could call an ambulance if he felt like it was needed. The call ended. By this time, I jumped off of the bed and ran to the bathroom. I was now vomiting. Preston called back to the front desk asking for an ambulance. He came into the bathroom to get me cleaned up and dressed. Since the ambulance had not arrived at our room by the time I was dressed, he picked me up and to the lobby we went. By this time, the ambulance had arrived. As Preston was getting into the ambulance with me, he looked up and saw Dr. Morgan. She asked what was wrong. He gave her a quick summary of my symptoms. She stated that she would meet us at the hospital if it was okay. Preston said yes, the ambulance doors closed, and we were off.

The next morning, I woke up in the hospital still in excruciating pain. As I scanned the room, I saw my sweet husband with his head lying on the side of my bed. He must have been there all night. I guess it was just overnight. I felt as if someone had just snatched something out of the right out of my body. Each time I tried to move, a terrible pain went through me. As I began to try and move around Preston awakened. He greeted me with a smile of relief. According to him I had been asleep for about four or five hours. I asked him what happened. He told me that I had experienced an intense pain, nausea, and passed out after I was loaded into the ambulance. According to Preston, Dr. Morgan performed an appendectomy because my appendix burst. All I could think was "Thank you God that Dr. Morgan was here, that my illness wasn't more serious, and most of all for sparing my life!" I was in the hospital for three days and then I was supposed to be released.

What a honeymoon! My appendix burst and I'm stuck in the hospital for five days! Whew, this was just too much! I rested comfortably for our remaining two days in Aspen. "I'm sorry Preston." "Don't you even go there! This was something beyond your control. I am grateful that you are alive." "Me too! Let's go home." As we were preparing to go home, Dr. Morgan came in. "I hate to be the bearer of bad news, but you can't go home yet. I need to make sure that you will recover properly so I want to keep you here another four to five days." "Are you kidding? Dr. Morgan we can't possibly stay that long. I have to get back to work!" I exclaimed. Preston placed his hand on my shoulder and stated to Dr. Morgan "We will be here as long as it takes to make sure that Mackenzie is okay." I gave him an eye of protest, but he wasn't hearing it. So I settled down.

The next few days were not that bad. The nurse had come in to assist me with a bath when Preston came in and the look on his face frightened me. I immediately became frightened. "What is it?" as Preston moved closer to me, he didn't look into my eyes he was focused on my body. I started looking at my body trying to see what he saw. "Preston what is it? You are scaring me!" "Where is the scar?" he asked. "Huh?" "Where is the scar?" he repeated. "What are you talking about?" I asked. "There is no scar? When you have an appendectomy, you should have a long scar on your abdomen. You don't have a scar." Preston turned to the nurse and stated "Get Dr. Morgan please." "Who?" "Dr. Morgan, the doctor who performed the surgery the night my wife came in by ambulance." "Sir, we don't have a Dr. Morgan here on staff," replied the nurse. "She's not on staff here? She is from Seattle. When my wife became ill and required surgery due to a burst appendix, she performed it. " "Sir, I can assure you that I don't know who that is." "How can that be?" I said to Preston. He just looked puzzled and announced to the nurse to start check out procedures because we were leaving.

Chapter 6

"Dead?" I couldn't believe what I was hearing. My baby is dead. The sound echoed through my head. Each time I heard it louder and louder. I couldn't believe it. There must be some mistake. "Oh God! Please let them be wrong!" The room started spinning and that's all I remember. I woke up in what felt like minutes; but it was actually two days later. I looked around and I was in the hospital. I sat up and my husband Steve embraced me. I sighed with relief. His embrace had always been so comforting and I needed him now more than ever. I pulled back and looked into Steve's eyes. His deep brown eyes were sad and I realized why I was there. "No! No! No!" Steve held me closer as I screamed until every ounce of my body hurt. My parents were there, but left the room to allow Steve and me to be alone. After what felt like hours, I was finally able to form the words "What happened?" Steve tried to explain what happened as best as he could. "There was a problem with the development of the fetus. Your body rejected it and you spontaneously aborted the baby." I couldn't bear to look at him anymore. What was he saying, spontaneous abortion? How can a mother's body reject her own baby? Steve continued to talk as I just sat there with my back turned to him. "Your body rejected the fetus because there was a deformity. If you had not rejected it, it could have killed you. "Celeste," (Steve's voice cracked. I knew I didn't want to hear this, but I just couldn't get my mouth to form a sound that could stop him from speaking.). The doctor doesn't believe that you will ever be able to get pregnant or carry a baby." I know I didn't hear what I just heard. He couldn't possibly be right. Not ever have a baby? I turned and looked at Steve. As he stood there like a lost little boy, all I could do was try to focus on what happened four days ago.

On December 1ˢᵗ, Steve and I found out that we were expecting. It was the best thing that could have ever happened to me. Me pregnant, a mother to Steve's baby, what could be more perfect? Our relationship wasn't always that great. Steve and I met when I was in medical school at Howard University. My schedule was tight. All I had time for was studying. The last thing I needed in my life was a man to complicate things. I was the first in my family to go to college. I was going to be the first doctor in my family. My mom and dad were expecting so much out of me. Sometimes I felt like running and forgetting about being a doctor. It was just too much.

Steve was there working on his master's degree in Chemical Engineering. He was in a fraternity. I didn't know much about pledging since no one in my family had ever attended college, let alone pledge a sorority or fraternity. I figured he was a womanizer so I wouldn't entertain his advances, but he was persistent if nothing else. He followed me around campus for a solid month. I wouldn't give him the time of day. He would constantly ask me out. My answer was always no, or I'm busy. He would often talk about things that he knew I would respond to. When I told him I wanted to be an Obstetrician/Gynecologist specializing in in-vitro fertilization, he would restrict our conversations to that only. To tell the truth, I was relieved when that was the focus of our conversation. That meant he was being serious. He didn't smile when he was serious. His deep brown eyes didn't dance when he was serious. There were times when I just felt the urge to just jump on him and kiss him. Oh this man was sexy beyond words. I had never been so attracted to a man in my life. My petite size and drive didn't seem to bother him. There was nothing about him that bothered me except when he got so close to me that I would just be drunk with the smell of his cologne. I had to keep a safe distance from Steve if I was ever to become Dr. Celeste Jones.

After a while, he gave up. It was a couple of days before I realized that I had not seen him around. The truth was I was so crazy about that man that I was terrified that if I started to date him and we broke up, I'd probably have to kill myself. That is never the answer, but I don't know which would be worse, my falling completely in love with him and end up dropping out of medical school, or not ever seeing him again, or even worse losing him to someone else.

I had always been told that I was a beautiful little girl. As I grew up I became even more beautiful, but I didn't appear to be getting any taller. I was teased something serious. When I entered middle school, the kids would see me and ask each other "Whose little sister is this? Shouldn't you be at the elementary school little girl?" I absolutely hated that, but what could I do? I spent many days crying and hiding. The only time I felt special is when I was in class. I always made A's and my teachers were very proud of me. Those idiots may have been able to tease me about my height, but they couldn't help but respect my brilliance. I made up my mind at that time that no matter what, I would always be the smartest. That would teach them a lesson. I didn't need to be tall to do that. Even if I weren't the tallest or the prettiest student, my mind would be phenomenal and my size or my height wouldn't matter.

One Sunday afternoon, I decided to look for Steve since I had not seen him for about two weeks. I figured he may be at his fraternity house, but I definitely was not going there. As I walked around the quad, there he was. As I moved toward him, he didn't see me. I was getting more and more excited the closer I got to him. All of a sudden a tall blonde walked up to him and gave him an envelope. He opened it and started to read the material. After he finished, he smiled and gave her a hug and a kiss on the cheek. I was crushed. I was too late.

I walked back to my dorm dazed. I don't know why I was so hurt. I had turned the man down more times than the number of students on campus.   I was almost in tears. I couldn't believe it. Now I would never know what it would like to be loved by what appeared to be the perfect man. I mean I had dated men before, but none of them showed an interest in my mind the way Steve did. Oh well!

I walked around campus until dark. I had lost track of time and my mind. I couldn't believe that I had wasted three precious hours walking around campus when I could have been studying. After I regained my composure, I headed back to the dorm. As I approached the front steps, there was Steve. I stopped in my tracks when he looked up at me. He smiled and said, "What's up stranger? Where have you been? I have been here waiting for you about two hours. You do come up for air, huh?" I was so confused. I was happy, relieved, and so scared all at the same time. I tried to act like I had not missed him. You know that didn't work, right? I tried to respond very causally. "Yes, I come up for air. What are you doing here? Are you lost?" Dang, I sound all wounded. I am, but he is not supposed to know that. He smiled. That was it. It was over. Steve stood up and walked toward me. He handed me the envelope I saw him with earlier. I was confused. "Open it." "What is this?" I asked. "Open it." He insisted. "Okay (with my eyebrows raised)." I read the contents. It was an application for a medical fellowship to the top in-vitro fertilization hospital in the country, Kennesaw University of Medicine in Aspen. I was speechless. I just stood there with my mouth open. I was absolutely frozen. "You're welcome." I looked up and Steve was standing so close that if he were any closer he would have been standing on top on me. As

I was about to say "You're welcome", he kissed me on the cheek and walked away. I stood there for what had to be two full minutes before I could move. When I realized what had happened, I started jumping up and down screaming "Thank you Jesus! Thank you Jesus! Thank you Jesus!" I knew then that I had to go find Steve. I turned around and started running toward his dorm. I rounded the corner and spotted him. I screamed his name. He stopped and turned as if in shock. When he realized that it was me, he smiled and moved in my direction. "I don't know what to say." "You said it with your eyes" he said. "Thank you!" That was all I could say. He said, "You're welcome." There was that smile. That was it. I was absolutely and completely in love with this man. I didn't even know his last name.

"Let me walk you back to the dorm. It's getting late." As he reached for my hand, I don't know what came over me, the next thing I know I had kissed him on the lips. He was so shocked that he didn't move. For a brief moment I thought I had done the wrong thing. We stared at each other, burst out laughing and shared the best kiss I had ever experienced. That was it, stick a fork in me, I was done.

With our crazy schedules I didn't think our relationship would last. I would always run when things were tough. Steve was determined enough for the both of us. He would push me and wouldn't let me give up, even when I was ready to give up on us.

After we dated for about a year, I was awarded the fellowship and had the opportunity to go to Aspen. I didn't want to leave Steve, but he insisted that I go. I had worked too hard and for too long to give up this opportunity. He held me close and kissed me deeply and said "CJ, I worked too hard to get you. You are truly my angel and I am blessed to have you. The only thing that will separate us is death. Celeste Jones will you marry me?" I stood there. Did I hear him right? Marry him? I stood there as if in a daze. He said "CJ, you can answer any time today." YES!!!!!!! YES!!!!!!!YES!!!!!!! I screamed as loud as I could. He then slipped the most beautiful diamond solitaire I had ever seen on my finger. It was for me and so was Steve.

I can't believe that was four years ago. How I wished I was there now, young and in love with a bright future. I had learned so much about helping women who wanted to get pregnant, how could this possibly be happening to me? My head started to spin. Steve held me to steady me. That was the only thing that kept my sanity. He held me so tightly and rocked me until I fell asleep. When I woke up, there was Steve right there holding me as he had done so many times before. Only this time, his embrace couldn't fix this.

A year passed and we saw the most renowned specialist in the country, Dr. Cofaxx. After he examined me, he gave us the news. My uterus was damaged and caused me to have a spontaneous abortion, a freak accident of nature happened. The only way we could conceive now was to extract eggs from my ovaries and sperm from Steve and have a surrogate carry our baby. If my uterus wasn't damaged, I could have delivered our baby, but that was not an option. The one thing that I knew about was in-vitro. I knew that through this process many women were able to give birth to their own children, but nothing could prepare me to undergo the procedure myself and not be able to deliver my own baby. Once again I was the little girl in middle school feeling inadequate and frightened. Steve reassured me that whatever I wanted to do, he would support it. If I had ever had any doubts about his commitment to our marriage and to me, it would never surface again. We agreed to begin the procedure. Since Dr. Cofaxx and I were colleagues he agreed to complete the procedure for us without charge. Money was no object. After all, I was an up and coming renowned doctor in my specialty, and Steve was an engineer and partner at his firm. We were more than capable of paying, but Dr. Cofaxx refused our offer to pay. Well, it was done. Since I couldn't deliver the baby, we would have to find an appropriate surrogate. I am thirty-four years old. I may not have much time left for good viable egg producing ovaries so we needed to move forward. We waited until the last year of my residency to get married. We waited three more years for me to get established and start earning some money before we started thinking about having children. If this is the only way, then it is. I will do whatever it takes to make our dream come true.

In-vitro fertilization is my area of specialty, but to go through the procedure yourself, definitely gives you a different perspective and gives you a deeper understanding of the hope that this procedure brings. I chose this field of specialty because my aunt, my dad's sister, wanted to have a baby but couldn't. She tried everything. She was married once, but she told me it didn't last because he wanted something that she couldn't give him, a baby. She once considered in-vitro, but it was too costly and he wasn't willing to go through the process. Eventually they stopped talking and soon he was gone. She often stated that she felt like she wasn't a real woman because she couldn't have children. After months of therapy she realized that having a baby did not define your womanhood. It is who you are; it's what's in your heart that defines you as a woman and determines your character as a person. At that time I was eight, but it had such an impact on me. Even though she said she was at peace with it, I don't think she was because I would often see sadness when she held the babies of one of her sisters. It was then that I decided that I would be a doctor to help women have babies.

There is little risk involved in this procedure, but there are so many factors that come into play to determine a couple's success. The woman's age and health play a huge factor. We needed to select the perfect person to carry our baby or babies. She had to be alcohol and drug free and physically fit to be able to carry and deliver our baby or babies safely. With the implanting of multiple eggs, I could end up with a small army, but I am okay with that, but the surrogate will have to be as well. How in the world can I convince someone to do that for me? I can't be worried about that now. We have come too far.

Taking a hormone injection to make me ovulate made me very emotional. For someone who doesn't mind using a needle and syringe on someone else, I thought I would have to get a sedative just to go through the first part of the process. Not to mention that my hip was sore from the injection. I was happy that I was going to be under mild anesthesia when they extracted my eggs. I know I would have been asking Dr. Cofaxx a thousand questions and I wouldn't have been able to relax. And honestly, I know it would have hurt beyond belief so I was glad I couldn't feel a thing. After it was over, of all the eggs extracted, I only had four viable eggs. I had hoped for more, but I'll take it. Waiting to hear if the eggs survived after fertilization was the longest five days of our lives. It took two to three days to determine if the fertilization worked at all and another two to three days to determine if the fertilized eggs had developed into blastocysts (embryos-babies). After that stage, then they could be transferred to a uterus to continue development.   It worked! Our blastocysts are good. All four of them are good. Since I don't have a uterus myself and I presently didn't have a candidate to transfer them to, they had to be frozen. They were healthy enough to wait for the perfect time.

We went through several agencies, but couldn't find anyone who fit the bill of someone we would trust to carry our children. It had been six months since we had the procedure done when I was at home after a long day lying on the couch when the telephone rang. It startled me. I jumped and realized that it had gotten dark outside. Where is Steve? I thought. I ran to telephone and picked it up. "Steve?" The voice on the other end was my mom. "How are you Celeste?" "I'm doing fine mama." "Is everything okay?" "Yes, why?" "I don't know baby. I just had a funny feeling that something was wrong." "No, mom. I fine. Steve should be home at any minute." "Okay. I just wanted to be sure you were okay. I love you." "Thanks ma. I love you too." Just as she said her last word, the doorbell rang. Lord Steve doesn't have his key. "Just a minute Stevie!" I hung up the telephone and ran to the door. I peeped through the peephole in the door and saw two police officers. I opened the door and stood there for a moment puzzled. "May I help you officers?" "Yes ma'am. Are you Mrs. Steven Morgan?" "Yes. What's wrong?" "I'm sorry to tell you ma'am, but your husband was killed in an automobile accident." I started to lose my hearing. I could hear a loud shrilling sound in my ears and then there was darkness.

It was a week later and I sat home alone in the darkness thinking. I had buried my lover, my friend, my soul mate. What do I do now? I have got to get out of here. I can't stay here anymore. I am going home. I called a moving company. Early the next morning, I had my house packed and the other items placed in storage. I locked the door, got into my Lexus sport utility and just started driving. Hours later, exhausted and grief stricken, I stopped at a hotel along the way, and checked in. I couldn't sleep or eat. I was lost and alone once again. Exhaustion finally kicked in. I put the Do Not Disturb sign on the door, and slept for fifteen hours straight.

Chapter 7

When Preston and I arrived at home my mom, sisters, and friends were there. My dad couldn't come. He had to work. They fussed over me and wouldn't let me do a thing. After a week, Dad, Maxine and Sandra went home. Mom stayed another two weeks. Finally I was my old self and mom went home. Boy am I going to miss them, but I will be more than happy to have this big house and Preston all to myself.

The morning after mom left, I got up and felt horrible. Preston offered to stay home with me, but I insisted he go to work. He had missed so much time from work already trying to take care of me that he needed to go to work. I felt nauseous and light-headed. After I laid in bed for another hour, I felt better and finally got up. I checked in with work and alerted them that I would finally be returning after being gone for three weeks. They were excited to have me back. I was excited to be going back.

The next morning Preston got up to get ready for work and I was sick again. Preston teased, "Mickey, don't pretend you're sick. It's time to hit the bricks sweetheart." He was standing by the bed when I threw up on his foot. Needless to say, he was convinced I was sick and a bit disgusted and irritated that I had just thrown up on his foot. He wasn't too sure that it wasn't on purpose. To tell the truth, I wasn't either. LOL! As he cleaned himself up, he came out of the bathroom with a silly smirk on his face. "What is so funny?" I asked. "Nothing. I hope you feel better. I've got to go. I love you." "Love you too!" After he left I got myself together and off to work I went.

I arrived at work and expected to see everyone standing at the door to greet me. I was excited about being back. I had missed them so much. I walked in with my million dollar smile, and all I got was "Hey girl! Where have you been?" I received that from everyone I saw. They were all cordial and I received some hugs, but not exactly what I expected. I picked up my face all the way to my office. I got married, got sick and have been out for three weeks and only one of them acknowledged it by asking "Girl, I know you were supposed to be out sick, but there was a rumor that you got married and left the country. I guess it wasn't true, huh? After all you are back here." She simply walked off. I felt my eyes welling up. I should have flashed my rock, but what's the use, they would probably think it was cubic zirconium. I went from being hurt to mad. I sat at my desk and got madder by the minute. I got up from my desk and went to the bathroom to get myself together. As I was getting ready to come out, Natalie came into the bathroom. "Hi MacKenzie! (with an air of pity) No she didn't! "Girl, how are you feeling? I was glad to hear that you were back." My eyebrows must have risen up to my hairline because that sister corrected herself quickly. "What I meant was, I had heard that you got fired because you were gone for so long." Well alright then. I was fired. No wonder everyone has those cheese eating grins on their faces. They believed I got fired and I was just allowed back. Well, I don't need this. I have a husband who loves me, and wonderful new life. I don't need this drama. "Thanks Nat, but I am fine." I started to move past her when she stopped me to give me a hug. I was thinking Lord help me. If this female does not let go of me I am going to go postal up in here. I thought she was the one true friend I had here. I guess not. Lord, I don't think I could take much more before I straight nut up in this place. Natalie released her embrace and I started to exit the bathroom when

Linda, the secretary came in. "Hey MacKenzie! Girl you better get out here. There is a good-looking man here asking for you. Girrrrlllll he is about a tall cool glass of water. Hurry up!" Okay, what clown is out here to see me? I know it's someone trying to sell the agency something that we are not going to buy or some loser trying to get me to convince his wife or girlfriend to come back to him because he has "changed". I am not in the mood for this on this day! I rounded the corner and headed to the front. When I arrived at the front, Maggie, the receptionist stated that she had shown the gentleman to my office. I took a deep breath and took off for my office thinking that Maggie had bumped her head and was rolling around on the floor for even having the thought that is was okay to show anybody to my office without my consent. I was getting more and more aggravated the closer I got to my office. I stepped into my office and my mouth fell open. There were flowers everywhere! I turned around to ask Maggie who sent them and there he was my love bunny. Preston of course! I burst into tears and ran to him. He smiled and embraced me. I was lost in his arms feeling sorry for myself when I heard a giggle. I turned around and the entire office and part of my church family were standing outside of my door screaming, "Surprise!" I thought I would pass out. They got me good. You could have bought me for a nickel and got change. They poured into my office hugging us and kissing us on the cheek and handing us gifts. Preston was grinning from ear to ear. Not once did he let go of me during our reception. This moment was priceless. We did absolutely nothing that day, but have fun! Boy did I need this.

Later that evening when I got home, Preston greeted me with a small gift. I was so excited I didn't even kiss the man. I squealed and tore open the gift. EPT. EPT? "Boy, what is this?" "A pregnancy test." "I know it's a pregnancy test. Why would you buy me a pregnancy test?" I got quiet. Then I looked at him. He was grinning like a Cheshire cat. "You think?" "Only one way to find out!" We ran into the bathroom.

Chapter 8

I finally emerged from my hotel room. I had eaten very little, had not combed my hair, and had not bathed but a few days during the two weeks I was in that hotel room. Now it was time to get on with my life without my Steve. What kind of life could this be without Steve? I didn't go home to my parents' house as planned. They would ask too many questions. I didn't have time for that. Instead I decided to go to a place where Steve and I went to visit a couple of years ago. A place where one day we wanted to live, raise a family, and start a practice. Seattle.

I set myself in motion. I needed to find a place to live and more importantly, I had to get back to work. That would help me get things back into perspective. As I scanned the telephone directory for a realtor, I came across a name that I knew, Alondra Venezuela. Yes, I think that's whom I will use. I contacted Ms. Venezuela's office to set up a time to meet with her. We agreed to meet that afternoon at 3:00 p.m. Alondra gave me directions to her office. The call ended.

When I arrived at Alondra's office building, I looked like I had been rode hard and put up wet. Alondra was startled by what she saw. "Celeste? Is that really you? What happened?" We had not seen each other in a couple of years so she was very surprised when she saw me and what terrible shape I was in. Steve and I met Alondra during a visit to Seattle. I have never been much of a talker, but we connected enough that I would consider her a friend. I had gone to a Mariners game with Steve and his college friends. We decided to go to a local bistro not far from the stadium for a late dinner. I was sitting alone at a table when Alondra came over to me and asked if she could sit down. I said yes. She sat down and we began talking about Seattle, life, marriage and our aspirations. I really enjoyed talking to her. We exchanged numbers and I stated that I would call her when we came to town. I did once or twice. We would see each other around town when we were there, exchange pleasantries, even chat a little, but we never established a close relationship, yet she is the closest thing I have to a friend in Seattle.

When I came into her office, I didn't appear to be doing too well; she invited me into her private office so we could talk. Alondra asked a few questions to determine what I needed, but from the looks of me, she knew what I needed the most was an ear and compassion. I was in my own world. I had not noticed that Alondra had moved from her desk and was now sitting beside me. She touched me very gently on my arm, which startled me. "Celeste, is there anything that I can do for you?" "Yes, can you help me find a place to live?" "It is obvious that you are grieving. How can I help you? Where have you been up too? I have not seen you since you were here with your husband." "I got up from my chair and walked over to a window that over looked the water. I turned my head ever so slightly and glanced into a mirror. I was horrified at what I saw. Tears began to form. I looked at Alondra and stated, "I need a masseuse, a hair stylist, and the way my eyes look, some Botox injections." Alondra couldn't help it; she burst into laughter. I looked at Alondra and followed suit. I shared with her what had happened over the past two years and that I just can't live in the house that I shared with Steve. There were too many memories and much too much pain. That's why I was here in Seattle, living in a hotel. I needed her to help me find a new home. She was startled. She had no idea what I had endured. We embraced and laughed and cried together for about an hour then I left. I had reconnected with a friend and that is what I needed. I was starting to feel like I was going to be okay.

As I was about to leave, Sharon, Alondra's business partner walked into the office. "Hi Alondra! Are you busy?" She saw me. "I'm sorry. I didn't realize you had someone in your office. I'll call you later." Alondra introduced us. We shook hands. "It's okay, I was just leaving." I said with a weak smile. I turned and said good-bye. Sharon stared at me as I left. She stood very quietly for a moment. Then she turned to Alondra and said, "She is in a lot of pain. All I could see was darkness, anger, and hopelessness." "You don't think she'll try to kill herself do you?" "No, I don't believe she will. She needs a lot of prayer and guidance during her time of grief." "Who did she lose?" You would think that this question wouldn't shock me, but it did. "Let's pray for her."

After my appointment, with Alondra, I went to the salon/spa she recommended. I had always worn my hair long because that was one of the many things Steve loved about me. I looked in the mirror and decided that it was too painful to look like Steve's wife any longer. "Cut it. Cut it short like Halle Berry, the actress." The stylist looked at me and said "Come again?" "Cut it short." She asked again, "Are you sure?" I took a deep breath and stated "Yes! Do it!" "Oookkaayy!" A couple of hours later, I looked into the mirror and I didn't recognize myself. My eyes were no longer sunken in; they looked bright and alive as I felt. My hair was fierce. It was short and significantly darker since all of my auburn color had been cut away. I was so excited I didn't know what to do. Yes I do. I am going to Disney World! I thought. No, for real I am going shopping. I am long overdue for a new look. But where will I put everything? I'll figure that out later.

I hit the mall with such a vengeance; you would think I

bought everything in the mall! If you could think of it, I bought it. I bought bags, scarves, jewelry, and oh the shoes. I had a ball. After the awesome spa treatment I had, I needed a make-over. After it was over, I was again taken aback at how much I was different mentally as well as physically. I had lost twenty pounds. My four foot eleven inch frame once again held an outstanding ninety pounds. I looked like a doll. I wasn't totally convinced at how breathtakingly beautiful I was until a young man in his twenties ran into a trash can staring at me. "I still got it!" I smiled to myself. Then me, and half the mall, went back to my hotel room. When I arrived and looked into the room, my doom and gloom awaited me. I immediately went to the telephone and called Alondra and made the announcement that I needed a condo or an apartment by 1 o'clock the next day. Alondra rose to the occasion. She loved a challenge. I jumped into some new pajamas, kissed my picture of Steve that I kept by the bed, and I went to sleep.

At 10:00 a.m. the next morning my telephone rang. When I answered a very cheerful voice responded "Are you ready to move?" "Yes!" I answered quickly. "I will pick you up at your hotel in twenty minutes" said Alondra. "Make it ten." "I'll be there." I jumped up, hit the shower and was ready to go in ten minutes as promised. When I emerged from the room, Alondra did not recognize me. This couldn't possibly be the woman she saw two days ago. I smiled brightly and jumped in. Alondra sat there with her mouth opened wide. "Good morning!" "Good morning? Who are you? I am here to pick up Celeste." "Girl, stop playing." "You look fierce!" "Yes, and I owe it all to you. Thank you for everything!" "You're welcome! Let's find a place for you to live." "Let's do it!"

Alondra took me to a prime location. We arrived at the newest condos in the Seattle area. We were in Buppyland. Buppyland is where the successful black people lived. It was in many locations around the Seattle area. It was just a matter of which location I would settle in. We went into a suite that had a master bedroom that was twenty by twenty, with a twelve by fifteen closet. With what I bought at the mall I needed to put my bed in the closet and use the room as my closet. It had marble floors and a fireplace. It was a dream. It had a total of three bedrooms, and two and half baths. The balcony had a breathtaking view of the mountains. This was perfect. I was home. Alondra took care of the arrangements for my things to be sent to my new abode in about a week. Alondra looked at me and asked, "By the way, are you still a practicing doctor?" "Yes, I am, but haven't had the heart to practice since I lost Steve, but I am ready to go back to work. So I need you to find me a prime location to start my practice here." "Well, alright then. I will spread the word!" Thanks!" The condo was ready to go and so was I. I knew I couldn't go back to the same hotel, so I temporarily moved to another location until my new haven was ready. After my last article of clothing was removed from my hotel, I looked around and said "Thank you Jesus!"

Chapter 9

Mrs. Sheila Kingsley is a wise and beautiful woman. She is seventy-five and as sporty as a twenty-five year old. She was so smart! She had the sweetest spirit of anyone I had ever met. She was soft spoken, firm and most of all truthful. She didn't ever tell you anything to hurt your feelings. She wanted everyone to deal in spirit and in truth. She said that this was the only way you could be free. I used to be afraid of her for some bizarre reason, but after I met her and spent time with her, I knew why everyone loved her and wanted to be in her presence.

Alondra met Mrs. Kingsley at The Holiness of God about two years ago. At her lowest point, Alondra went to the altar for prayer. Mrs. Kingsley held her hands and started to pray for her. When Mrs. Kingsley let go of her, Alondra knew that she had to make some changes in her life. Mrs. Kingsley told Alondra things that only she and God knew. All the money she paid to counselors over the last six months, Mrs. Kingsley did for free in ten minutes. She was finally ready to hear what they had told all her along. It took Mrs. Kingsley to help her accept what she needed to do. Alondra would be changed forever. She knew without a doubt that God heard her prayers, that He loved her, and He wanted to bless her, but there were some things that she needed to do. She spoke with Mrs. Kingsley often. She learned how to pray and hear from God for herself. Her life has not been the same. She is truly blessed! She knew that it was no coincidence that she came to The Holiness of God Church of the Living Word. After she started reading the Bible and trusting that God would heal her broken marriage as well as her broken heart, she believed she could be free. Even though her marriage didn't work out, she knew that once she believed in Christ and was obedient to God's Word, the world she knew would be forever changed. She was right. She became employed as a realtor in an establishment for which she became a partner in two short years, she no longer had to see a therapist, and was now in a relationship with a gentlemen who treated her the way she should be treated, like a queen.

Alondra and I met at The Holiness of God Church of the Living Word on visitor's day. She was the one greeting new comers on that particular Sunday. We hit it off right away. We would often speak after church and after a while we started to go to lunch together. Since Alondra had been in the Seattle area for about three years, she was an expert of what was available in the area. Lorna took me to her church, helped me find a dentist and a hairstylist. Alondra also uses Dr. Morgan and recommended her very highly when I asked how she felt about her. Dr. Morgan started her practice a couple of years ago when her husband, Steve, died in a car accident. Since the start, her practice was doing very well. Her clientele was a mixed array of women from different ethnicities, mainly from middle to upper class, and sometimes wealthy. She recommended her to me when I asked if they were any gynecologists of color in the area. Alondra wouldn't have dreamed of sending me anywhere else. Not only was Dr. Morgan of our ethnicity, she was the best in what she did. Alondra knew we would hit it off. She thought we needed each other.

Alondra is a low-key kind of person. She is spiritually grounded, has her head on straight, and has many friends who genuinely like her. She is smart and well- educated. She became a real estate broker after her marriage ended. Her marriage had been horrible. Her prince charming turned out to be a drunken wife beater. Alondra was the typical textbook woman who was being abused. In fact, she felt as if she wrote the book. She made excuses for his anger. She was willing to accept anything he dealt at her as long as he didn't leave her so she kept her abuse a secret.

When she started attending the Holiness of God Church, she was praying that she would find a reason to live. If she made her husband angry, he would beat her. That was her life. She wears a scar across her left brow that reminds her that she is a child of God. The scar represents how much God loves her, and saved her from the clutches of death. And even though, her new beau, Sebastian loves her, the scar represents a love no man can ever give her. Alondra didn't know where things started to fall apart. She met Joshua while she was in college working on a nursing degree. She had always wanted to be a nurse and work in pediatrics. Joshua was in medical school. She thought he was the most handsome man she'd ever laid eyes on. He had a very light creamy complexion. His mother was white and his father black. He had green eyes that appeared to look through to your very soul. She considered herself blessed that he would even look in her direction. Alondra has a dark smooth complexion. She had jet black hair and oval shaped eyes. She looks like a black China doll. She never thought she was pretty enough because of the nicknames she was given as a child that never reflected on her brilliance or beauty. Others could only see her dark complexion. Now she had a man who appeared to be very much in love with her; all of her and she was willing to do whatever she had to keep him. She learned the hard way the true meaning of doing anything to keep your man.

Joshua was working hard in medical school. He was under a lot of stress. He became angry if Alondra wasn't there to help him do research. He had no regard for her needing to study for her own career. He was such a smooth talker that she would eventually give in to help him. No doubt her studies suffered.

After a couple of semesters of failing grades, she was kicked out of the nursing program. Alondra was devastated. Of course Joshua came to the rescue. He promised her that he would make it up to her. It was his senior year of medical school and he was offered a job in Seattle, Washington. He asked her to marry him. She said yes. She'd been waiting for a year for Joshua to propose; now that he had she wasn't so happy. Her gut told her to run. She shrugged it off to just feeling scared because she was kicked out of school, was about to be married, and move away to a place where she knew no one. Alondra was accustomed to the people in Atlanta, Georgia. It wasn't far from home, and she had many friends there. Now she was going to Seattle, Washington. That was a long way from Georgia, but she was willing to go to be with her man. Once in Seattle things immediately became worse. Joshua became angrier and more verbally abusive. Alondra stood up for herself at first, but after he hit her in the face and broke her nose for refusing to clean up the bathroom when she was sick, she knew that the only way she would be free of him was for one of them to die. She knew she couldn't kill him, so she planned to kill herself.

Joshua had gone to school. He was on a tirade before he left. He screamed obscenities and even spit in her face before he left. The man who once sang her praises now treated a dog better than he treated her. How would she do it? Would she cut her wrist? Would she overdose? Could she run herself off of a cliff? It would be just her luck, she would become paralyzed and he would put her in the worst nursing home possible. She started to cry. She wasn't allowed to cry in his presence, but Master Joshua wasn't home and she cried uncontrollably. She cried until she vomited. She cried so her ribs hurt. Her head hurt. Her eyes hurt. When she thought she would lose her mind she screamed "God please help me! I don't know what to do anymore. I tried everything I know how, but nothing works! I can't do this anymore. Please help me!" She lay on the bathroom floor and cried until she fell asleep. When she woke up she was in the hospital. Her head was bandaged and she had an excruciating headache. As she tried to place her hand on her head, the nurse turned and welcomed her back among the living. Alondra had no idea what she was talking about, welcome back. Welcome back from what? "Excuse me nurse, what happened?" "You don't know do you? You were involved in a car accident?" "A car accident?" "Yes. The doctor and the police will want to see you." Doctor yes, police why? She thought as she lay there thinking that her head was about to fall off. The police came in along with Dr. Reggae. "How are you feeling Mrs. Venezuela?" "My head hurts, and I don't appear to be missing anything, so I guess that's pretty good, huh?" Dr. Reggae smiled and said "Good. The police would like to speak with you about the accident. Do you feel up to it?" "Sure. I don't know how much help I would be since I don't remember having an accident." Sergeants Gomez and Smith entered and introduced themselves. Sergeant Gomez began to speak, "Mrs. Venezuela I need to ask you a few questions about the accident. Can you tell me what happened?" "No I can't. I don't remember being in an accident. The last thing I remember is that I was at home upset, crying on the floor and falling asleep. That's all I remember." "Ma'am I hate to have to tell you this, but your husband is dead. He died at the scene of the accident." Did he say dead? Joshua is dead? How? When? Oh God, what happened? "Ma'am? Ma'am?" I was in a daze. I wasn't sure I heard him correctly. Joshua is dead. "Officer, what did you say?" "I'm sorry ma'am. Your husband died at the scene of the accident." I just laid there stunned. I couldn't believe what I heard. Joshua was dead. I cried like a baby. Although he had beaten me senseless and had treated me like trash, I didn't wish death on him. He wasn't saved. I wouldn't wish death on anyone especially an unsaved soul, no matter how much he hurt me. I cried.

I stayed in the hospital for three days. While I was there,

Mrs. Kingsley visited me. My family flew in from Georgia. My mom and dad agreed to stay with me until I was better. I loved them for the offer, but the last thing I needed to do was go back home to the house that I shared with Joshua. I asked the doctor if I could travel. He stated that if the trip was short, I got plenty of rest while I was there, and I followed up with a doctor in Georgia he would release me. My parents assured him that I would get the rest I needed and see our family physician, Dr. Thomas, as soon as I reached Georgia. I was going home as soon as I able to go. But first things first, I had to lay Joshua to rest.

I had to identify Joshua's remains. I was wheeled downstairs to the hospital morgue. That was the hardest thing I had ever done. I positively identified his body. I was shocked when I saw his face. I wasn't sure what I would see. His face was untouched by the accident, but it still had a look of pain and anguish. I felt so much sadness for him. When I was asked when the funeral home would be picking up his body I realized that his parents may not know that he was gone. I told the attendant that I would make a call and he should be picked up by tomorrow. I would have to call them and let them know. I dreaded making this call, but I knew that I had to tell them. How would I tell them that their son died while trying to kill me?

I called the last known number I had for my in laws. His mom Estella answered the phone. I had not spoken with my mother-in-law in a long time so I wasn't sure what to expect. His parents lived in Miami. That's where they moved to when Dr. Venezuela retired. "Hello Mrs. Venezuela. This is Alondra." "How are you?" She said very dryly. "I am fine. I am sorry to have to call you, but something has happened to Joshua." "What? Where is he? Is he hurt? Let me speak to him?" she insisted. "I'm sorry, but Joshua and I were in a car accident and he didn't survive the crash." "What are you talking about? We spoke with Joshua last week. What have you done with my son?"

she screamed. "Mrs. Venezuela, I am so sorry. Can you come to Seattle? I am arranging to have a funeral for him by the end of the week." "Don't do a thing until we get there." She hung up. I sat there and stared at the telephone in disbelief. I didn't expect the call to be pleasant, but I was most definitely not expecting that reaction.

When the Dr. and Mrs. Venezuela arrived, I had been released from the hospital, but I was not able to meet them at the airport because I was still recovering from my injuries. They came to our house demanding information. My parents were there and intervened. Joshua's mom accused me of hurting him and demanded that there be an autopsy to verify his cause of death. I shared that an autopsy was already completed and that I had the report. Mrs. Venezuela insisted upon seeing it. My parents protested because of her behavior. My parents were trying to remain calm because the Venezuela had just learned of their son's death and were trying to process everything that had happened, but so was I and they had had just about enough of the verbal abuse of Joshua's mom. Dr. Venezuela was very calm and offered me comfort despite his wife's outrageous behavior. I asked my mom to give Dr. Venezuela a copy of the autopsy. He read it and looked at me with sadness. He understood what the report said. He knew that his son was drunk beyond the legal limit. He also knew that his son was abusing drugs. He looked at me and apologized for his wife's behavior and insisted that they leave so I could rest. Dr. Venezuela stated that he would call tomorrow to find out the details of the funeral. Just as his wife was about to get started again, he ushered her out of the house. Once they were in the car, he explained to her what he had read in the report. He shared that their son was drunk and under the influence of drugs when the accident occurred. For a brief moment Mrs. Venezuela sat quietly. She remained quiet as they traveled to the hotel because she refused to stay in the house with me. Not that she had that option. Dr. Venezuela could not understand her behavior. He knew that she was upset about losing Joshua, but he knew that her behavior was bizarre even for her.

As they were preparing to go to bed for the night, Mrs. Venezuela shared what she had been thinking in her quietness. She had developed the scenario of what happened the night her son died. She shared with her husband that if her son was that drunk and high it was because I was driving him crazy trying to make enough money to support his gold-digging wife. Dr. Venezuela looked at his wife as if she had grown a second head and was speaking a language not yet identified. He knew that she thought her son hung the moon, but he was now convinced that she was absolutely out of her mind. He didn't know what happened the night of our accident, but he knew it was not at all like what his wife envisioned. In her mind I was driving. We had an argument and I became so angry that I decided I would kill him by running him into a tree for the insurance money. There was one thing wrong with her theory, I didn't know about the insurance policy. Doc just sat there amazed at how far her mind had taken her without any information at all. To settle her for the night, he assured her that he would get a police report to find out what happened. She said she wanted a full investigation because she had plans to make sure I paid for what I had done to her baby. The doc just shook his head in disbelief. He didn't care what she did as long as she would lay down and be quiet so he could deal with his son's death without listening to her accusations against me and her criticism of how he was not handling their son's death the way she thought he should be handling it. Mrs. Venezuela was always a force to be reckoned with if things were not to her expectation. During the early days of our dating, Joshua shared with me about his relationship with his mom. No matter what he did, he didn't measure up to his dad's greatness or her expectations for a son. According to Joshua she was hard on him. She often talked down to him and would resort to corporal punishment if she deemed it necessary. Dr. Venezuela was rarely at home because of the long hours he worked at the hospital, so Joshua had no one to protect him.   On the rare occasions that she called after we were married, I could hear Joshua answering her as if he were still a little boy who was about to be punished. I never understood Joshua until this very minute. I thought to myself…."The apple didn't fall from the tree." Joshua was just like his mother. Even though his dad was there physically he was never present for him emotionally. There were times when his dad would try to do things with just him; his mom would somehow find a way to interfere. Mrs. Venezuela's constant rejection and criticism molded Joshua in a way that he never even knew. I finally put the pieces together.   I was going to make this funeral as quick as possible because my monster-in-law had to go.

I had a graveside service since I was still recovering from my own injuries and Joshua didn't have any real friends. Dr. Venezuela was very supportive of me, but Mrs. Venezuela tried to make the service an ordeal. She needed all the attention to be on her and how she was suffering as a mother. At the end of the service she even tried to faint. It was like watching a movie. She stood up, her right hand went flat against her forehead, palm facing out, and then she fell over the coffin. She almost knocked it off of the stand. I was absolutely amazed. I know you are thinking that I should have been upset at this scene by his mom, but I just couldn't be. I would have been upset if she had bothered to have any tears during her performance. I guess, as she got older she couldn't command tears the way she used to command them. During this performance, Dr. Venezuela never moved. When I looked at him, his eyes were big and his eyebrows were raised, but he never made a move in her direction. He allowed the funeral director and attendants to manage her. After I regained my composure from watching her theatrics, I felt sorry for her. I wondered what her life must have been like when she was a child. I also wondered how in heaven's name he had put up with her for all those years and if she was always so entertaining. Mrs.

Venezuela and I never had a good relationship and I am pretty sure that it was not about to happen at this point.

Joshua was lowered to his final resting place. I watched intently as he was lowered into the ground and knew that once and for all my life as Alondra Venezuela was over. No one truly knew what my life was like. I hid it well, except from Lorna. Lorna and I weren't the best of friends, but she knew me well enough to know that something wasn't right. She had encouraged me to leave before the abuse became physical, but I didn't listen. I guess it's too late now, huh?

The Venezuela's were leaving immediately after the funeral. Her evilness just looked past me as she moved to the car they had rented while they were in town for the funeral. Dr. Venezuela stopped and expressed how sorry he was for all that had happened. He stated that he would check on me from time to time, but he regretted not doing more to help Joshua deal with his childhood demons. I was taken aback by this statement. What did he mean? He leaned down to take my hand. He kissed my hand as he had done so many times before, but this time he paused and looked at me. I smiled and looked at his face as if to etch it in my memory when I noticed a scar on the left side of his face near his ear. I had never noticed it before today. I guess I never really saw it before this day. He knew exactly what I had endured.

The trip home was pleasant. My parents waited on me hand and foot. It was wonderful. This was exactly what I needed. My first three nights I slept peacefully, drug induced peaceful, but peaceful nonetheless. On the fourth night, I decided not to take as much medicine. It helped me sleep, but I felt lousy when I wasn't asleep. "Lord, what happened on the night of the accident?" I lay down and drifted off to sleep. As I slept everything became clear. I was lying on the floor in the bathroom and didn't hear Joshua come back in. All of a sudden the door swung open and there he was mad as usual. "Get up! Didn't I tell you that I wanted this house clean? Is this what you do when I'm not here? What do you have to cry about? You have a beautiful house and more clothes than you can wear in a year without wearing the same thing twice. You ungrateful witch! You want a reason to cry? Let's go!" "Where are we going?" I screamed through tears. "What? Are you questioning me? Get up now!" "Okay. Let me put on some clothes. No, when I say get up, I mean now!" He dragged me outside and pushed me into the car. He didn't push my head down as he pushed me into the car. My forehead hit the corner of the car and gashed my left brow. I screamed in agony but he didn't respond. He jumped in on the other side and tore down the street. I was screaming and holding on for dear life. He was screaming and cussing. "I should just run into a tree and end your miserable life. You have got it made and all I ask is that you keep the house clean and you can't do that!" "Give me one good reason why I shouldn't kill you right now!" He was looking at me in a way that terrified me. Then it happened. I saw a large truck headed straight for us. I screamed for him to stop and look out for the truck. He smiled and asked "Or you'll do what?" He stared at me and then…it was two days later. As I lay there dazed the words came to me as clear as day, I will never leave you nor forsake you. I was struggling with the fact that Joshua was gone. That he was in so much pain and so angry that he was so beyond reason to a point that his life ended while in the process of trying to end mine. I wanted to be free of Joshua, but didn't know how to be free. I never wanted death for him, but it appears that this may have been his plan. He had planned to end his misery and take me with him. "Thank you God for your mercy and grace."

Chapter 10

"What does that mean? Read the box boy!" "Congratulations Mrs. Stone. We're pregnant!" "Pregnant?" "Pregnant?" "Pregnant?" "Yes baby, you're pregnant!" I screamed to the top of my voice! We held each other and cried. "I can't believe I'm pregnant? Who do I tell first?" "Whoa! We won't tell anyone until after our appointment confirming that you are pregnant and know the expected date of delivery." "You mean I can't even tell my mom?" "No, you tell your mom and you might as well as have alerted CNN because all the free world will know that you are pregnant." "You are wrong for that!" "You know I'm telling the truth," he said laughing. "Okay. You have a point. I'll hold it until after the appointment." "Good girl!"

The appointment went well. Dr. Morgan stated that the baby was due October 2nd. Preston and I had all of our friends over and made the big announcement. Everyone was ecstatic. We can't wait until baby Stone makes his/her entry into the world. I immediately began making plans. I picked the room that would be the nursery. I can't wait to find out the sex of the baby.   At our initial visit, we stated that we didn't want to know the sex of the baby, but by my sixteenth week of pregnancy, we couldn't wait any longer. Every four weeks we go to the doctor to check my weight, and to measure my abdomen to determine the growth of the baby. When you reach your sixteenth of pregnancy, an ultrasound is performed to look at the baby's development and confirm the child's due date based on its size and development. You also listen to the baby's heartbeat.

We listened to the heartbeat first. It sounded like windshield wipers on steroids. It was very, very fast. We laughed when we heard it. The nurse smiled and then she commented that I had gained about ten pounds since last month's visit. "Is that a lot of weight?" I asked. "Yes! Dr. Morgan will talk with you about it when she comes in. Often when you gain a lot of weight, it could be a sign of gestational diabetes, but don't worry." Now we're worried! While the nurse was completing the ultrasound and explaining to us what we were seeing, suddenly her mouth dropped opened and she stated that she needed to get Dr. Morgan. "What's wrong?" Preston and I said in unison. "Nothing, I'll be right back. I need to get Dr. Morgan." Preston held my hand as we waited for Dr. Morgan. Dr. Morgan came in quickly. The nurse whispered and pointed to the screen. Dr. Morgan smiled. Preston and I were about to pass out with anticipation. "What?" I asked. Dr. Morgan smiled and reassured us that there was nothing wrong. "Preston and MacKenzie, I'm sorry the nurse frightened you, but she wanted to be sure of what she saw. There is an excellent reason why you are gaining so much weight. You are pregnant with fraternal twins." "Twins?!?! We're having twins?!?! We said in unison. "Yes, twins. There is one there," she said as she pointed to the screen of the ultrasound, and "there is the other. They are in separate embryonic sacs. It appears that this one is a boy. See the turtle? The other one is a girl. See the hot dog bun?" To say that we were surprised is an understatement. We were teary eyed and in utter disbelief. "I can't believe we're having two babies!" I looked at Preston and said, "Well, I guess we know how to decorate the nursery now, huh?" Preston responded. "Yes, I guess we do. When can we tell everybody?" I asked. "Let's keep it a secret. Let's at least let that be a surprise." Preston said. "Okay, okay I guess we can keep some things a secret." I said reluctantly. "There is one thing that is definitely not a secret." Preston stated. "What's that?" I asked. "How much I love you and that you have made me the happiest man in the world!" He kissed me passionately. Smiling, the nurse interrupted our moment by saying "Hey, that's how you two got here!" We both burst into laughter.

Dr. Morgan couldn't help but admire them, picture perfect, like her and Steve. She quickly left the room. When she went to her office, she pulled out a picture of Steve and wept uncontrollably as she held his picture to her chest. "Steve, I hoped it worked." She then picked up the telephone and made a call.

The months passed by quickly. I was spoiled rotten. Preston waited on me hand and foot. He made sure I didn't want for anything or do anything. When I reached about thirty-four weeks, I had to stop work and was restricted to bed rest. This is typical for women carrying twins. I was elated about the impending birth, but I was miserable. Let me just put it out there…rest has nothing to do with bed rest. I had to lie in one position day and night. There was so much pressure on my bladder that I literally had to roll out of bed every hour to go to the bathroom for a trickle of urine. My bladder was reacting as if there was a gallon of fluid waiting to be free. Ugh! We had chosen the names for our sweet babies. The girl would be Madison and our little man would be named after his dad, Preston, II. I couldn't wait for Madison and Preston the II to arrive. The nursery was ready. The nanny that would help me once the babies were born was ready and in place. The only thing needed was my babies.

Preston was unsure of how to care for a baby, let alone two babies. When he had to go and live with his grandparents he was grateful he was the only child because of the love and attention he received. He knew he could handle one child. That child would have everything it needed including parents that would only have to care for him/her. As he thought about it, he realized that if I was pregnant with twins, it was meant for us to have two children. I was thirty-two and he was thirty-four when I got pregnant. We got a late start having children. He's probably thinking we are too old to have any more children after these two, so he should be safe from having to do this again. He is absolutely correct! I am good! I am not trying to look like a grandparent at my child's graduation.

On the morning of September 12th I didn't feel well. As Preston was getting ready to leave, he noticed that I looked very flush. He placed his hand on my face. I was burning up. I just thought it was normal. I had been feeling bad for a few days, but knew I would because I was so close to delivery. Preston went to the bathroom for a thermometer. That man knows he will get a thermometer in a heartbeat. My temperature was 101.7. He immediately called Dr. Morgan's office to alert her that I was sick with a high fever. Preston was instructed to call an ambulance to transport me to the hospital and that she would meet us there. Preston called my parents and arranged for them to fly to Seattle immediately. They assured him that they would be on the next flight to Seattle. He was scared and he wanted them there to make sure that everything was good.

My mom and dad arrived at the hospital later that night to find out I was not only running a high temperature, but my blood pressure was also running high- 160/100. Dr. Morgan recommended that I have a cesarean section immediately. Dr. Morgan ordered the nurse to call the operating room and alert the neonatal intensive care unit of the pending arrival of my premature babies. Preston and I were terrified. "Shouldn't we wait until you can get my pressure down?" I asked. "I'm sorry we can't wait that long. MacKenzie, I don't want to frighten you and Preston, but if I don't take the babies now, none of you have a chance of survival." Preston and I looked into each other's eyes. We were both crying at this point. Preston stroked my cheek, "MacKenzie, I love you and our babies. I know God didn't allow us to get this far to take everything away from us. We must have faith that God will see us through this. We must have faith that the three of you will come out of this well. I have to believe that the Lord is with us always and that he will never forsake us. MacKenzie, do you believe that the Lord knows best for us?" "Yes!" "Do you believe that everything works together for the good of those who trust in him?" "Yes!" "Let's pray."

Dr. Morgan entered the room, followed very closely by a nurse. "Preston. MacKenzie. It's time. Preston asked when he would be getting dressed to go into the delivery room. Dr. Morgan touched Preston's arm gently and stated "Preston, due to the nature of this surgery, you can't go into the delivery room." "What? I have to go. MacKenzie needs me. My babies need me!" "Preston, MacKenzie needs you calm and praying for them. I promise I'll come out and speak with you as soon as the procedure is over." Preston thought that request was strange, but he reluctantly agreed. In the child birth classes, he never heard that there may be a circumstance that would not allow him to be present for the delivery of his babies even if it's for a caesarean section. He held my hand until he couldn't go any further. He kissed me and reassured me that everything was okay and then I disappeared through the double doors. Preston looked at Mr. and Mrs. Clay and said, "They're going to be okay, right?" Preston was on the verge of falling apart. He fought to regain his composure and he started praying. My parents were praying too. Mr. Clay was on one side of Preston. Mrs. Clay was on the other. They held on to one another for the entire procedure without uttering a word.

Dr. Morgan moved quickly. She had no time for an epidural. She used general anesthesia. She had to move quickly. My temperature was rising higher. If she didn't get my babies out, I might have a stroke and she could lose all of us. There was too much riding on this. Dr. Morgan was short-tempered with the nurses and the surgical team assisting her. The team was taken aback; this was very unusual behavior for Dr. Morgan. She was usually very calm, even in dire situations, and that's what made her one of the best obstetrician/gynecologist on the Pacific Northwest coast. She continued to bark out orders throughout the forty-five minute procedure. Everything appeared to be going well. Baby one arrived without incident. Madison Dianne Stone arrived weighing four pounds and three ounces. Preston David Stone, II, on the other hand was having major respiratory problems. He made his entry into the world with his cord wrapped around his neck and abdomen. He was considerably smaller weighing in at two and a half pounds. Both babies were rushed to the neonatal intensive care unit. Both babies were examined. Madison appeared to be okay. Preston was still struggling. After Dr. Morgan had closed the incision, she went out to share the news with Preston and the Clays. Upon hearing the events of the surgery, Preston was relieved that I was okay and that I was stable. He praised God that Madison appeared okay. He prayed to God that baby Preston would be okay and that he would be healed. Neither Preston nor my parents were allowed to see any of us for about two hours. They were the longest two hours of their life.

After speaking with Preston and my parents, Dr. Morgan went to her office and collapsed. She was so emotional that she could no longer contain her composure. She had almost lost everything in one moment. What if they didn't make it? She couldn't allow herself to think of that. It was more than she could bear. After she regained her composure, she came back to check on me and then she would check in with the pediatrician to see how our twins were doing.

Dr. Wallace, the pediatrician that we chose to care for our children, was in with Preston and I and my parents when Dr. Morgan came in to check on me. Preston and I both were very emotional. Dr. Morgan became alarmed. "Dr. Wallace is there something wrong?" Dr. Wallace stated "Baby Preston is not doing well. I am not sure that baby Preston is strong enough to survive." Dr. Morgan nearly fainted. She became so light headed that Dr. Wallace had to catch her before she hit the floor. He sat her in a chair next to my bed. Preston came to her aid as well. "Are you okay Dr. Morgan? Please know that you did all that you could do for us. We thank God for you." I didn't feel quite the same. As I watched Dr. Morgan I wondered to myself why she was so emotional about our babies. I had an eerie feeling. I didn't know what it was, but something wasn't right. From the expressions of my mom and dad, they also appeared to be wondering why she was behaving in such a bizarre manner. They never said a word.

Preston went up to check on the babies while my mom and dad stayed in the room with me. Madison looked like what you would imagine an angel looked like. She had a few tubes attached to her, but she was still the most beautiful little girl he had ever seen. Gorgeous black curls covered her little head. He thought she looked just like me. He saw baby Preston close by. His small frail body had several more tubes than Madison, but he was so handsome. He didn't know who he looked like, but he was handsome. As he stood there and stroked his hand through the incubator, he knew that this was good bye. He wanted me and my parents to see him. He asked the attending nurse if I was able to go to the nursery. She said yes. I was allowed to go to the nursery in a wheelchair. My parents followed very closely. We entered the nursery while my parents stood outside of the nursery and waited for us to come out. When I saw baby Preston, I too knew I was saying goodbye to our angel. Preston and I touched him together. We thanked God through our tears for allowing us the opportunity to touch an angel. Dr. Wallace came in to share baby Preston's prognosis. We looked at him, smiling through tears. He knew that there was nothing more he needed to say. We asked if we could hold him. Dr. Wallace told the nurse to unhook him. We held him for the first time. We kissed him gently, called him by name and continued to praise God until he went home to be with the Lord. We held him and each other and cried. Preston helped me stand from the wheelchair. We walked over to Madison's incubator and introduced her to her brother. We promised that she would know about him when she was older. After another thirty minutes, we allowed the nurse to take him. We touched Madison, and praised God for her health. Preston helped me sit back down in the wheelchair. He wheeled me out of the nursery. We didn't have to say a word. My parents hugged tightly through their tears. My dad told Preston that they were going to go to the waiting room to give us some time alone. Preston insisted that they go back to our house to spend the night because he was to spend the night with me at the hospital. They forced a smile, got a key to the house from Preston, and headed to our house. Preston wheeled me back to my room. After Preston tucked me in, he couldn't help himself. He tucked himself in next to me and we held each other gently and cried ourselves to sleep.

Chapter 11

I still can't believe that Joshua is dead. When I got back to Seattle from my parents' house, I alerted the police of what I remember about the accident. All I ever wanted was for Joshua to love me for me. I never dreamed that things would end the way they did. Each time I looked at the scar on my face it will serve as a reminder that the Lord loves me and has great things in store for me.

I remember returning to Seattle, still shaken about everything that had happened, Mrs. Kingsley came by to see me. She hugged me and told me how much she missed me. She had a look of concern on her face. "What is it Mrs. K?" "Alondra, you have been through a lot. I know you don't understand everything that has happened to you. Please know that God loves you. Please know that God loved Joshua. Joshua turned his back on the Lord. He refused to hear from Him. He blamed the Lord for the way his life turned out. The Lord tried to warn him several times that he was living contrary to His will. That's why he never had any peace or joy. He wouldn't turn from his evil ways. He tried to destroy you and ended up destroying himself in the process."

I realize even now that I still have a lot of healing to do. I know that the Lord will fully restore my mind, body, and soul as evident on how He had moved in my situation with Joshua. Through all of this, I know what faith means. That is a lesson that I will not ever have to learn again. I also know now that I don't have to settle. If there was ever to be someone in my life, if he didn't truly love God and know how to treat a woman, then I won't have anything to do with him. I know that now with Sebastian. I love him, and believe he truly loves me. However, before we progress in our relationship, and future, I know I still need counseling. I am still dealing with Post-Traumatic Stress Disorder (PTSD). I will call MacKenzie and set up an appointment with one of the counselors where she works. I am ready to move on with my life. I am ready to move past the death of Joshua. I want to breathe again. I want to live among the living. I am not sure how much counseling I will need, but I trust that the Lord would help me through this process and it will end when it is supposed to end. I don't know who I am, but I want to. No one has ever asked me what I wanted. I wasn't sure that I could answer that question if someone asked me. One thing that I know for sure is that I want to know who I am and more importantly who I am in Christ.

As I sat, deep in my thoughts, the phone rang. "Hello." "He didn't survive. What am I going to do? He didn't survive!"

Chapter 12

D r. Morgan couldn't believe Preston Stone, II, had passed away. When she heard this, she lost all the color from her face and fainted. She was out for several minutes before she awakened. She couldn't believe what she'd heard. Baby Preston was dead. This couldn't be possible. What had gone wrong? She kept going over the details of the births over and over again in her head. What went wrong? She had failed to save her son. She would do whatever she had to do to make sure that her daughter survived. She went to the nursery to check on Madison.

An autopsy would be performed on baby Preston and then we could lay our son to rest. Dr. Wallace came to see me. I was in a suite near the nursery. I refused to leave the hospital without my daughter. Madison was doing well and would be able to go home soon. Preston wasn't there when Dr. Wallace spoke with me. "Mrs. Stone, are you expecting your husband soon?" "Yes. What's wrong with Madison?" I asked. "Nothing, please don't be alarmed. Your daughter is doing fine." "Then what's wrong?" I asked again. "I don't know how to tell you this, but baby Preston is not your son." Did I hear him right? What does he mean, Preston is not my son? How can that be possible? I looked at Dr. Wallace and asked "What do you mean, he's not my son? He was delivered by cesarean section minutes after Madison. You have to be wrong!" I was becoming more and more upset by the minute. I felt like I was going to faint. I needed to call my husband. Preston had gone home to get more clothes for me, shower and change clothes, and check on my parents. I was expecting him to return within the hour. I couldn't wait that long. "I need to call my husband." Dr. Wallace left the room. He answered the home telephone on the second ring. "Hello." "Preston!" I was almost yelling. "What's wrong MacKenzie? Is it Madison? MacKenzie?!" "Preston, you need to get back here now!" Preston dropped the telephone back on the cradle and headed back to the hospital with my parents close on his heels. When they arrived, they found me on the verge of hysteria. "What's wrong baby? Please tell me!" "Preston, Dr. Wallace said that Preston is not our baby." "What? He spoke so loudly, MacKenzie jumped. That can't be possible. Where is Dr. Wallace?" he asked. "I don't know," I answered. "Where is Madison?" he asked. "She's in the nursery." "Where is Dr. Wallace?" "I don't know, but he's in the hospital somewhere." "MacKenzie, stay calm. I'll be right back. Mom and dad, please stay with her." I was a mess. I couldn't believe it. How can the worst experience of my life become even worse? My mom and dad were trying to make sense out of what was going on, but I was in no shape emotionally to explain it. They just tried to reassure me that everything would be alright. I rang the buzzer for a nurse. "Yes ma'am?" "I need to see Dr. Morgan?" "Ma'am Dr. Morgan hasn't been in since you delivered." "Thank you." I looked at my parents and said "I have a sick feeling." Where is Dr. Morgan? Why had she responded the way she did about my babies delivery? "Lord, I know I haven't always turned to you unless it was in time of trouble, but when I have needed you, you have never disappointed me. I thank you for who you are in my life. There is something wrong, please show it to me Lord." We all said amen.

As we were saying amen, Preston returned with Dr. Wallace. "Dr. Wallace, my wife has shared something bizarre with me. Please tell me how my wife can give birth to a child and you tell us that he isn't ours? That is impossible! How could you make such a mistake? With all the medical advances available to man, I do not accept what you are saying. Are genetics your area of specialty?" "No sir, it is not." I want a genetic specialist to perform a complete genetic make-up on my son and daughter. You better pray that you are right and have not caused us unnecessary grief and pain." "Mr. and Mrs. Stone, I know that this is difficult to hear, but please try to stay calm. I don't believe it myself. There is no way that Preston is your child. Mr. Stone, your blood type is A-. Mrs. Stone, your blood type is A-. Preston's blood type was O." "How can that be possible? Preston came from her body immediately after Madison." Preston was beginning to lose his cool. He could no longer contain his confusion, his anger, or his grief. He couldn't take much more. He wanted to cry, but couldn't for my sake. "I need the tests taken care of immediately." "I will take care of it Mr. Stone." stated Dr. Wallace. "Never mind, I got this." Preston announced. Preston was standing close enough to my bed that I could touch him. I reached out and touched his hand. He looked at me, kissed me on the forehead, and announced that he would be right back. Dr. Wallace was at a loss for words. He stated that he wished that he had different news, but he didn't. He apologized and left the room. He left us to process the information he shared. With all that was happening I forgot that my mom and dad were in the room. When I looked at them, they just stood there and appeared to be in shock. My dad came to my side and said "Baby, I don't know what's going on, but I know in my heart that everything will be okay. Preston is a good man and great lawyer. Let him do his thing. When I gave you to him when you got married, he promised me he would take care of you. I believe he will. You should too. Get some rest and try not to worry. Mom and I will go back to the house now so that you can rest. By the way, when are we going to be able to see our granddaughter?" I smiled and said that she should be out of the neonatal intensive care unit by tomorrow." "Good, I am ready to start spoiling her!" my dad exclaimed. My mom laughed and said "Me too!" My dad said "We will wait until Preston comes back and we will go back to the house." "Okay. Thank you for being here. I love you."

All of a sudden it hit me, what is Madison's blood type? I motioned to get out of bed. My mom stood up from the couch and said "Where are you going? You do know that you have had major surgery and you need to be careful don't you?" "I need to get to the nursery." Moving ever so slowly, I went to the nursery to look at Madison's blood type. Lord, what will I do if her blood type is not A-? I couldn't take it if she isn't mine. Please let her be mine was all I could think as I walked to the nursery. My mom waited outside as I went into the nursery. As I was approaching the incubator, my heart was racing and I could barely breathe. I looked at Madison's birth card…blood type, A-. "Hallelujah Jesus!!!!!!!" I was crying so much, the nurses thought something was wrong. I reassured her that everything was okay. What a relief! As I watched our beautiful daughter, I noticed that she appeared to be sucking on her nasogastric (NG) tube. This tube carries medicine and food to Madison's stomach through her nose. "Nurse, she appears to be sucking." Is that normal?" The nurse smiled. "Yes. That's normal for a little one who is ready to eat. After two long days, the moment had arrived, Madison could be held and breastfed. My poor mom was standing outside the nursery door waiting anxiously to find out what was going on. I finally came out and shared that everything was okay. My mom sighed a breath of relief. I told her she could go back to the room because I was about to try and breastfeed Madison. She was so happy. She gave me a hug and a kiss and headed back to my room. I know my dad was probably wondering if he needed to send out a search party for us.

Breastfeeding is not what I expected. Madison had a hard time latching on initially, but once she got the knack of it, it was all good…for her. I loved the fact that I could feed her, but it was quite painful. The nurse told me that the girls would be sore and particular areas would be dry and cracked after each feeding if I did not apply an approved amount of ointment to the affected area. I wanted to give up, but I didn't. The nurse told me it would get better, but I wasn't so sure. After my initial attempt at feeding Madison, the lactation nurse tried to teach me how to retrieve my milk by using a breast pump. Once the machine started pumping I almost came out of the chair. I was sure that once the suction cup came off, I was missing something that I started out with before the pumping began. Either I will do it the natural way or not at all. Natural it is.

Preston returned just after my first attempt at feeding Madison. I wondered why he had been gone so long. He shared that he had to make some calls and that we needed to discuss arrangements for baby Preston. We had received permission to bury him. He stated that he would alert the family of when and where the service would take place. We decided Preston David Stone, II, would be laid to rest on Wednesday at 10:00 a.m. He walked me back to my room. We told my parents when the funeral would happen so that they could alert the rest of the family. We didn't want anything big, just Preston and I, my parents, and my sisters if they can make it. We weren't prepared for the grief of burying our precious son. We are even more determined to find out the truth of what really happened, and why Dr. Morgan suddenly disappeared.

All the family gathered for a graveside service to include my sisters. (Thank God they were able to come. I needed them there with me.) It was short and sweet. I asked Mrs. Kingsley to stay at the hospital with Madison so that I and my parents could attend my son's funeral. We didn't trust anyone at the hospital. Madison was set to go home on Thursday. Preston and I were happy that one of the happiest moments was about to happen, taking Madison home. And yet, it was also bittersweet. As we were making plans to take Madison home, we were also making plans to say goodbye to our son. After the service, my family had to go home. My mom and dad had been with us for six days. I was extremely grateful for their presence, but it was time for them to go home. I was ecstatic that they had the opportunity to see Madison before they went home.

Home! We are finally home. I am happy to be home and ready to settle into a routine. The nanny was on point. The baby was in the room with Preston and me for her first night. What a sweet sound, to hear a baby cry. I insisted upon being the one to get up each time Madison sang out. I wanted to do everything for my daughter. This lasted for about three days before sleep deprivation kicked in. Preston tried to get up every time I got up. He wanted to change her diaper and then give Madison to me to feed. He watched me feed her for the first couple of times. After that he was so exhausted he didn't hear a thing after the first night. LOL! After Madison was lying in her cradle beside our bed, I slipped off to sleep. When I slept, I had a vision. I was in Aspen on my honeymoon. I saw this woman in a mask with a syringe. I woke up in a cold sweat. The words that I heard in my dream came back to me, "the woman in the mask is not what she seems". "Lord what does that mean? Where is Dr. Morgan? Why hasn't she been back to check on me since she delivered the babies? Something is wrong, Lord. What is it?" I peeked at our sweet princess sleeping soundly in her cradle. I smiled, but the thoughts of my dream kept playing over and over in my mind. I couldn't shake it. I would have to have answers to my questions and I knew where I needed to start, with Dr. Morgan.

Chapter 13

I was resting peacefully at my parents' house when I heard the telephone ring. A few minutes later, my mom alerted me that it was for me. When I answered, it was a Mr. Whittingham from Mutual Life Insurance. "Mrs. Venezuela?" "Yes." "I would like to start by saying that I am sorry for your loss. The primary reason that I am calling is to determine if you want your money direct deposited or would you like a cashier's check mailed to your current location?" "What check?" I asked. "Your husband had a whole life policy worth one million dollars. It also pays double indemnity in case of accidental death." "Are you asking me what I want you to do with two million dollars?" I asked. "Yes ma'am that would be correct." I swallowed hard and requested that the check be mailed to my parents' house certified and overnight. The call ended. I was in shock. I couldn't form the words to speak my mom's name. Within ten minutes of the phone call, my mother walked into the room. She saw the look on my face and became concerned. She grabbed my hand and asked "What's wrong baby?" "I looked at her with watered eyes? "Alondra, what's wrong?" "Momma, that was the Whittingham Mutual Life Insurance Company. They are sending me a certified check for ...." "For what?" My mom was now standing. "For two million dollars!" I started screaming. My mom started screaming. We both began to praise the Lord. "Thank you Jesus! Thank you Jesus! Thank you Jesus! You answered my prayers Lord. My wait was not in vain. Praise your name my God!" We cried and screamed; we praised God and danced until I got dizzy. I weaved a little before I fell on the couch. My mom grabbed my hand and said "Baby are you alright?" "Yes mom I'm fine. I just over did it. Momma, we are wealthy. We will not ever lack again." I smiled from ear to ear.

My check arrived the following day. Lord how do I deposit two million dollars? There's only way to find out. As I prepared to leave, there was a note in the envelope with the check. It simply read….

I know this money in no way makes up for what happened to you, but I hope that you can use this to start putting your life back together. This policy was purchased after you and Joshua were married. His mother was supposed to be the beneficiary, but I changed it to be left to you before the documents were returned to the insurance office. Despite all that you endured, you were good for Joshua. I had hoped that the love of a good woman would calm his anger and give him the validation he needed, but I should have known that it wouldn't. I have to be honest; it was the love of a woman, his mother that caused him to behave the way he did. No matter what he did, he could never please his mother and I think that is what he saw in all women. I am so sorry for your pain and pray that you will be able to forgive me for not getting my son the help he needed or sharing this with you before. Have a good life. I will be sure my wife doesn't bother you ever again. Dr. Peter Venazuela.

I sat there stunned. This explained a lot. That's why he wanted the death certificate. It wasn't so his wife could prove that I had done something to cause her son's death, but to ensure that I received the money from the insurance policy that he had.

My mother and I arrived at the bank promptly at 9:00 a.m. the following morning. I chose the bank that I thought also had a branch in Seattle. When I inquired about accessibility from Seattle, what I heard was a little disappointing. This particular bank did not have a branch in Seattle, so I made a deposit to my parents account in the amount of five hundred thousand dollars. I asked that the rest be returned in a cashier's check so that I may deposit it once I returned to Seattle. The bank was more than happy to oblige with the kind of money being deposited. It would take a few days for the check to clear and then I would receive my cashier's check to deposit once I got home. I couldn't have been happier.   Neither could my parents.

I prepared to go home. My parents were going to miss me, but they knew it was time. My body had healed and it was time to go home and take care of unfinished business. The first thing I will do is contact the police about the accident, and then I will have to decide what to do with the house. There were too many ugly memories in that house. It will have to go.

When I arrived in Seattle at 1:00 p.m. I immediately went to the bank to get all of that money out of my hands and safely into the bank. I then took a taxi home. I was leery of what it would be like to walk into what was once my prison, free. I didn't know what emotions would await me, but I knew I was about to find out.

When I arrived and walked through the house, I could smell his presence. Each and every room reminded me of the hell I had gone through for two years. Everything would have to go. I started with my closet. All of the clothes that he selected for me over the years were the first to go. You talk about having a "Waiting to Exhale" moment? I packed up every bit of it. I wanted to burn them because I didn't want any other woman to have to wear the clothes of a woman who felt less than worthy of life, but I decided that wouldn't be a good idea. The new Alondra was here to stay. I took all his clothing, shoes, and coats and boxed them up and contacted the Salvation Army to pick them up. All of the furnishings, everything would have to go as well. I put the house on the market. Everything that Joshua and I shared would have to go. I knew that my healing would not truly begin until I did. "Thank you Jesus! I'm free!!!!!!!!!!!!" Then I started to dance. I danced harder than I did when I received the money. Alondra Venezuela was on her way to restoration.

I couldn't believe where my life once was and where it is now. I am in love with Sebastian, a man I met while working toward my real estate license. My real estate business is successful, and I am living the life. I was excited about my business trip to Nevada. I loved looking at new properties and wanted to branch out, but not sure if branching out this far from home is wise. I will have to obtain a realtor's license in another state, make connections with people I don't know. It is risky, but I am willing to take a chance. As my plane is preparing to land, I looked out of the window and see the Grand Canyon. "Wow! I am in Las Vegas. This should be a blast!" After I take care of business, I will go back to Seattle and continue moving forward. Come to think of it, Dr. Venezuela did a life changing act of kindness for me so I need to pay it forward. The plane landed and I went to the luggage terminal. After I picked up my luggage, I powered on my cell phone and made a call. "Hello Celeste. I think I know how to help you."

Chapter 14

I surfed the World Wide Web about postpartum depression. I wanted to complete the check list so that I would know if I am exhibiting symptoms. With all that I have been through, I thought I needed to do some reading. I am very emotional. I was scared that something would happen to Madison all the time. I was afraid to let her out of my sight. I thought of baby Preston often. My heart was broken. At night when things were quiet, I drift off to sleep and see his face. I can smell him. I would wake up crying. I felt lost. I felt vulnerable. I have a healthy baby girl that I need to take care of, but I can only concentrate on my loss. I don't want to go out or see friends and family. I don't eat unless I absolutely have to eat. I sometimes struggle with how I am going live with the pain of losing him. It is starting to consume me in ways that I haven't recognized. I only feel at ease when Preston is home. I need him to reassure me that everything is okay, but he can't. The one thing that he can't give me is our baby boy. I need to get help to deal with my loss because I feel like I am about to lose my mind. There are times when I think I have, but I know I can't stay here in this place. I have to learn how to move forward. I need to do what I need to do. I need to see a counselor. I may even need medication, but I will do what I need to do because as I said, I know I can't stay in this place, emotionally and mentally vulnerable.

As I surfed, I had an urge to go to Dr. Morgan's website. I had never visited the website before. I wasn't sure that there was a website. What I read on her site absolutely astonished me. Dr.

Morgan shared what happened to her that prevented her from having children, becoming interested in studying in vitro-fertilization, losing her husband and how she had planned to someday have a child with the husband that she had lost. "If I can't help one woman in the miracle of life, all of my work will not be worthwhile," Dr. Morgan stated. The mask; the syringe……. "Oh my Lord, was Preston her baby? Does she believe that Madison is hers?" My stomach began to hurt. I feel nauseous and thought I was about to lose the contents of my stomach. After I sat and thought and thought about the events of that day, I began to get angry. The angrier I became, the more upset I became until I was crying uncontrollably. "I've got to call Preston."

Before Preston could leave the office his telephone rang. It was me. I was very upset and he couldn't understand what I was saying. He tried several times to calm me down, but to no avail. He hung up and headed home. He sped across town like a mad man. All kinds of things went through his head. Was I sick? Was Madison sick? "Lord, please let everything be okay. I don't think I'll survive if I lose one of them! Please Lord, help me!" Please help me Lord was all Preston could say all the way home. Suddenly a peace came over him. He knew that something was wrong, but he refused to believe that the Lord gave him this beautiful family to take it away from him now. Preston started talking to the Lord saying whatever he was about to encounter that the Lord was going to get us through it. That was his last thought as he reached home. I came running out the house into his arms. He held me close afraid to breathe. He loved me so much he thought he would go crazy. (That's what I'm talking about!) He loosened his embrace and looked into my eyes as we stood in the garage. "What's wrong?" "Preston, when we were in Aspen, do you think it was a coincidence that Dr. Morgan was there?" "What?" he asked. "I don't think it was a coincidence. "I said. "I don't know what to think MacKenzie!" "Preston, baby Preston wasn't our baby. I think Dr. Morgan placed her eggs in my uterus while we were in Aspen." "What?" Preston asked with a bewildered look on his face. "Preston, where is my scar from the appendectomy?" I lifted my shirt for him to examine my abdomen. No scar. "I know that has always puzzled me." said Preston. There was a small scar above my naval and that was the only scar I had. Preston's head started to ache. He couldn't believe what I was saying. It just couldn't be true. If it were, how could it be proven? Who would believe such an outlandish story? He didn't and he was living it. There had to be a way. Preston decided he needed to start his questions with Dr. Wallace.

It has been two months since Madison made her entry into the world. It was time for her to go and see the pediatrician for her two-month checkup. The first month we went in every ten days because I was breastfeeding and he had to make sure that she was gaining the proper amount of weight. Trust me she was. I feel like my shirt was off more than it was on the first month of her life. After her two-month checkup we went home and Madison took a nap. While she was napping I called Dr. Morgan's office. To my surprise, an answering service responded stating that Dr. Morgan had taken a temporary leave of absence and all her patients are being referred to Dr. Matthew Kendrick. She could at least have had the decency to be in her office when I call so that I can get the answers that I needed. I decided to call Dr. Kendrick and set up an appointment. The nurse that answered stated that she would call back with an appointment time as their office had been flooded with calls from Dr. Morgan's patients and they would need time to obtain medical records before she scheduled an appointment for me. Then a fleeting thought entered my brain. Dr. Kendrick's office must have some kind of communication with Dr. Morgan or at least have access to my medical records. I stopped the nurse before she could hang up and asked what were the possibilities of my gaining access to my medical information? She stated that she would provide an electronic copy of it as soon as she had access to it. The call ended.

Finally, maybe I can figure out how all of this got started. One thing was for sure, I had to start at the beginning, Aspen.

Chapter 15

My thoughts went back to where it all began. I am sitting in front of the home where Steve and I began our lives together in Aspen, Colorado. I can't sell the house. I can't. I sit in the driveway and just stare at the house, lost in thought. How could things have gone so wrong? My life wasn't perfect. I had had disappointments, experienced a broken heart, and lost my husband and children. My son didn't survive his birth and Preston and MacKenzie are raising the other baby. I have to get my baby. That is all I have left of Steven and there is nothing that can keep me away from my daughter. I began to rock slowly as I sat quietly. The longer I sat, the more I cried and the more I rocked. I must have been there for hours. All of a sudden, I realized I was cold and hungry. "Where can I go?" After I sat there for another fifteen minutes, I decided I would go to my parent's home.

I am exhausted, but decided I am okay to drive the three and a half hours to my parent's home in Denver, Colorado. I won't call my mom to let her know that I am coming because she will be worried and call my cell phone every 15 minutes until I arrived. My brain is on auto-pilot. I had no idea I was home until the motion censored lights outside of my parent's house came on. It startled me for a moment. I gained my composure and went to the front door. I was determined that I was not going to cry and get my mom and dad all up in arms (good luck with that). As soon as my mom opened the door and saw my face, she just grabbed me and held on tightly. My dad was not in the same room when I arrived so he had no idea what was going on when he entered the room. He didn't ask any questions, he just closed the front door and embraced both of us. After about ten minutes, my mom gently guided me to my old room, helped me get undressed, and tucked me in. In the meantime my dad went out to retrieve my luggage from the car and make sure it was locked before we settled in for the night.

I slept for about fourteen hours before I emerged from my room. The thing that stirred me the most was the smell coming out of the kitchen. I smelled all of my favorites. I smelled turkey bacon and coffee brewing. I was never a fan of coffee, but the smell meant that mom is cooking in the kitchen, dad is sitting at the table reading the paper waiting patiently, and everything is right with the world. But it isn't. Nothing is right. Steve, baby boy Morgan is gone, and baby girl Morgan is with someone else. I feel depression looming in the room. I was overwhelmed with my sense of loss. I needed to turn that energy into getting my daughter back. What should I do first? First things first; "I need to eat." I headed to the kitchen.

I was greeted by hugs from mom and dad, but I was also greeted with the look of "What's really going on?" I was in no mood to rehash everything that had happened so I put on a good face, smiled, and said, "I'm fine. Mom let it go…for now."

Chapter 16

I continued to get stronger every day. Returning to work was what I needed to distract me from the craziness in my life. Business is good. I had missed working at Healing Hearts while I recovered. While there was plenty of work to keep me occupied I couldn't help but wonder how it all got started. Why did this happen to us? How is Madison? A smile appeared on my face. As I sat and thought, there is a knock on the door. It's Alondra. What a sight for sore eyes.

Alondra asked me how I was and what she could do to help. I said, "Help me find Dr. Morgan." Alondra was taken aback, but agreed to do what she could to help locate Dr. Morgan. I needed answers if I was to ever have closure. I asked Alondra if she knew any private detectives that could help me. She stated that she would look around and see if she could come up with someone that could be trusted and that would get the job done quickly. That gave me hope. "Now, what about lunch? I hear that the restaurant down in the harbor is having a special on shrimp and I thought I heard them talking to me as I drove to your office." I started to laugh and agreed to go to lunch.

While at the restaurant, I went to the bathroom to wash my hands and I bumped into the woman coming out the bathroom. We smiled and said excuse me like you often do when you nearly run into someone else. I went in and washed my hands and returned to my table without giving the near collision another thought. Alondra and I had a filling, delicious lunch.

The only thing we needed to do after our meal was go home and take a nap. I was beginning to feel like myself for the first time in a while. We separated at the restaurant and each of us went back to work. Alondra picked up her cell phone and hit a number she saved on speed dial. "Hello." "She wants me to help her find a private investigator." There was a long pause. "Hello. Did you hear me?" "Yes, I heard you. Delay her as much as you can." "Okay." The call ended.

After a long afternoon at work, I was finally headed home. I drove and thought. I had my favorite CD playing, Fred Hammond's Nothing But The Hits. I was singing along and feeling good. My mind just floated as I continued my drive home. When I arrived, Preston was still at work. I headed straight upstairs to see my sweet Madison. Madison would light up whenever Preston or I came into the room; this made our hearts melt every time it happened. I looked forward to it. It was about 6:00 p.m. Preston will be home in a couple of hours so I have plenty of time to feed, bathe, and get Madison ready to see daddy when he comes home. Like clockwork he arrived at 8:00 p.m. ready to get to his sweet Madison. He walked in and said "Where is my Maddie?" She lit up and started to fall in his direction. He loved on her for about 30 minutes until she was ready for bed. He kissed her once more, whispered I love you, and gave her to me for her bedtime feeding. I was as ready to breastfeed her as she was ready to be breastfed. Since I had returned to work, Madison has to take mommy's milk from a bottle all day long so she is happy to get milk straight from the factory before she goes to sleep for the night. After the feeding was over, I went in to get settled for the night. Madison was no longer eating in the middle of the night, but going to bed early is essential for me. I have to be rested because she is ready to eat at 5:00 a.m.

As I prepared for bed, Preston was in the kitchen eating and sorting through the mail. When he came to the bedroom to get ready for bed we talked about our day. I shared that I had a good day at work, but was happy to be home. He shared the same sentiment. I shared that I had asked Alondra to help me find a private detective to find Dr. Morgan. Preston sighed heavily. I asked, "What was that about?" "I want to find Dr. Morgan as much as you do, but please don't allow her to become your focus. She has obviously gone into hiding. Finding her will not be easy and I don't want you to lose you while you are trying to find her." I was tired and obviously misunderstood his reaction. "So, you are saying I won't find her so I shouldn't try?" I asked. "No, that is not what I am saying." responded Preston. "It was what I heard" with my voice now slightly elevated. Preston knew this was not where he wanted this to go, so he just said, "MacKenzie, I'm sorry. That is not what I meant. I pray that we find her because I want to know what happened as much as you do. I know you are tired and the last thing I want to do is add to your grief, BUT please remember that I lost my son too." And with this statement, he exited the bedroom to cool off. I sat stunned and started crying. For once, Preston did not come back to comfort me, he needed his own comforting.

Preston had not had a drink since college, but at this particular time, he felt like he was overdue. He went to his man cave and found a bottle of Black Label Jack Daniels that he discovered a few months ago. It was a wedding gift. He had it tucked away for a special occasion. He found his Jack Daniels glass that came with it. He went to the fridge and filled his glass with ice. He poured himself a drink. He had been able to hold it together for months; to be strong for me, but at this moment, he was done. He took a sip of the Jack Daniels and cried. All the anger, pain, and grief that he had stored up, was released. He was alone and he no longer had to be strong for anyone.

It was about 2:00 a.m. when Preston woke up and realized he had fallen asleep in the cave. He felt lighter and needed to check on his girls. He first went to Madison's room. She was sleeping peacefully. She looked like a doll. Chubby cheeks with a head full of curly black hair; she had his heart from the time he realized he had a daughter. He could just stare at her forever, but he knew that he needed to go to bed if he had any chance of getting up and going to work in a few hours.

He then entered the master bedroom. I was in bed with my back turned to the door, but I wasn't asleep. Before he could speak, I rolled over, sat up on the bed, and began to apologize for overreacting. I went on to say that I had been so wrapped up in my own grief that I had forgotten about his and for that I was truly sorry. I asked if he would go to grief counseling with me. He said yes. He sat on the bed, laid his head on my shoulder. He smiled tenderly, crawled into bed and we held each other until morning. We had gotten very little sleep, but knew we needed to go to work. I stated that I would find a counselor for us. He stated that it sounded good and that he was open for anytime. We dressed for work, greeted the nanny, gave hugs and kisses to Madison and then to one another, and went to work exhausted.

I found a counselor who could see us on Tuesday of next week at 3:00 p.m. I was just about to call Preston to let him know when the appointment was when my telephone rang. It was my assistant letting me know someone was there to see me. I told her to send her in and hang up. There was a small knock on the door, before I could say come in, I looked up to see the woman I had almost run into at the restaurant.

"Hey, don't I know you?" "Yes, my name is Alyson Smart" she responded. "Nice to meet you. Please have a seat." I said. "Thank you." she said. "How can I help you today?" "I am here because I have something for you." "For me? What is it?" I asked. I was handed an envelope. I opened the letter, read it, and looked at the deliverer. "Is this a joke?" I demanded. "No ma'am. Consider yourself served." I looked at it again. We were being sued for the custody of Madison. What kind of sick joke is this? I just sat there. I kept reading the same lines over and over again. Once my brain allowed me to process what just happened, I continued to read the rest of the letter, I noticed that the person who was suing us is…yes… you guessed it, Dr. Morgan. "Really? She is suing us? O! It's on!"

Chapter 17

I remained at her parents' house for about three weeks. I didn't leave the house for a solid week. I stayed in my room and slept. I continued to replay in my head everything that had happened up to this point. I was suffering from depression only I had not realized it. I was so consumed with getting my baby that I hadn't noticed that I had not left the house in many days.

"Okay, enough of this. I need to get moving. I have been away from my baby for too long. It is time to bring her home." Celeste decided that she was finally ready to leave the house. She picked up her IPhone. Since her mood around her parents appeared to have lightened, they stopped asking her so many questions. Celeste was far from being okay. She searched for an attorney. She finally found an attorney that specialized in paternity cases. His name was Mr. Lawrence Thompson. He agreed to meet with her the next day for a consultation.

Celeste met with Mr. Thompson. The story she told Mr. Thompson was that Dr. Stone agreed to carry her babies and then decided to keep her daughter when the other twin died. Mr. Thompson was startled and appalled at what he was hearing. He stated that he would take her case. In her mind, MacKenzie had been a willing participant. MacKenzie was the right age and had the perfect physique to safely carry and deliver her babies. She was a newlywed in her thirties who was planning to have a baby soon anyway so she was willing to help her. Celeste had created in her mind a conversation where MacKenzie had actually verbally agreed to give birth to her babies. She had lost it. She was starting to have delusions. She had actually convinced herself that her baby had been stolen.

Mr. Thompson told her that he would start the paper work immediately. He stated that he would get a court date to petition that the custody of baby girl Morgan be immediately given to Celeste until absolute paternity could be determined. She was happy and thought that her nightmare would soon be over. She left Mr. Thompson's office and headed back to her parents' house. When she arrived, she was in the best mood she had been in since she had arrived. Her mom was so excited to see her baby starting to look and act like herself. They ate dinner and Celeste retreated to her room.

Celeste started looking for baby furniture and clothing for her baby girl. She would have to guess on the size since she had not seen the baby since birth. She was so excited. She made sure that she kept what she was doing a complete secret from her parents. She didn't want them to know that they had a granddaughter and that their grandson had died. There was so much she needed to tell them, but she had to wait until the perfect time. Until then, she would plan, order her baby's things online and have them delivered…where? It had not occurred to her that she would have to decide where she and the baby would live. All of a sudden she burst into laughter. "Oh my goodness! My baby needs a name! What will I call her? I can't keep calling her baby Morgan, huh?" Laughing again. Then it came to her, Stephanie Celeste Morgan. She then looked at a pink dress in a magazine and stated "Stephanie, you are going to love this!" She continued to laugh and plan for the next three hours. She had lost all track of time. She was snapped back into reality when her mom knocked on the door to ask if she was okay. She quickly stated that she was and that she was getting ready for bed. Her mom offered her something to eat, but she stated that she wasn't hungry. Her mom retreated.

Celeste's mom shared how happy she was that Celeste was home to her husband. Mr. Jones looked at his wife and said "Honey, I am happy that Celeste is home too, but something is wrong. She really hasn't been right since Steve died. She refuses to talk about it or see a counselor. She shows up here unannounced looking lost and now she's fine? She stays in that room, except to eat. No, she is far from fine." "I know, but I just couldn't accept that something may be wrong with her." Mrs. Jones began to weep. She looked at her husband and asked, "What should we do?" "The first thing that we are going to do at the first chance we get is look in that room and see what she is hiding." Mrs. Jones agreed. The Joneses settled down for the night. Operation – What is Celeste doing?- is now in operation.

Chapter 18

My first reaction was to cry, but instead I got angry. I started to play back in my head all that Preston and I had gone through and I got angrier and angrier. I picked up the phone and called Preston. This time I was not crying or being hysterical. I was matter of fact and completely focused. I told Preston about the summons, and told him if she wanted a fight, a fight she would get. Preston didn't know who this was, but he liked her. He had not seen this side of her in a long time. He didn't tell her that he had hired a private investigator. Not yet. He wanted to have all the facts before he told her. She couldn't wait to get this situation settled. "Boy, if I ever needed Olivia Pope of Scandal, it is now!!!"

We met with Mrs. Latricia James-Miller. She was a Christian Counselor. She specialized in helping people deal with grief. I hoped that she could help me deal with my anger because I was fit to be tied. Mrs. James-Miller didn't make us wait long. She introduced herself and allowed us to do the same. She asked that we share what our goals were for counseling. I stated that I wanted to be able to work through the hurt and anger that I felt about losing my baby and the anger I was still feeling toward the person that caused all of it. I was about to get really turned up when Preston touched my arm. I didn't realize that I had raised my voice and was sitting on the edge of the couch before he was able to get my attention. Now, it was Preston's turn. Preston shared that he was dealing with fear, anger, and was having a hard time dealing with trying to be strong for me.

Mrs. James-Miller shared that she planned to help us through our grief. She shared that in her office we were safe and needed to deal in complete honesty.

Before we began the session, we held hands and prayed. After prayer was over, Mrs. James-Miller asked Preston to look at me and asked him to share how he feels about losing Baby Preston. Preston looked at me and stated, "When I lost Baby Preston, I was completely devastated. My heart ached. I couldn't breathe. I felt like I wanted to scream, cry, run...my emotions were all over the place, but I couldn't because I needed to be strong for you. As your husband and Madison's dad, I am supposed to take care of my family and I am struggling to do that. I want to let go of my pain. I don't want to be angry anymore. I just want to live happily ever after with you, Madison, and any other babies that we may have. I play what happened in my mind over and over again until it makes me sick. I mean physically sick. I don't want to carry it anymore. I don't ever want you to think that I am weak because I am not, but I need so much to let go of my pain and anger." By the time he spoke his last word, he had tears streaming down his face. He was trying to keep himself from completely falling apart. Mrs. James-Miller looked at me and instructed me to tell Preston that it was okay to let go of the pain and anger. I, crying too, stated to Preston, "It's okay to let go of the pain and anger. I want to let go of it too." We were both relieved. At this point, Preston cried. He finally felt safe enough to cry in my presence. He was. As he cried, I was the one holding him and reassuring him that it was okay. The session ended with a prayer. This is what we needed.

This session started our healing process. We knew healing would not come over night, but at least we had a start. We met with Mrs. James-Miller for six more sessions. Our conversation went from our hurt and pain to our anger about the documents we received concerning custody for Madison. We had obtained a lawyer to guide us through the legal process. Mrs. James-Miller offered us the opportunity to deal with whatever emotions we were dealing with in order to be prepared for what was to come. We were ready.

After our sixth session, we went home, put Madison to bed and settled in for the night. We felt closer than we had ever before. We felt as if we know each other and could support each other better than before than when we started the sessions. I dropped off to sleep with Preston snuggling me from behind. Suddenly, I was in an operating room; there was the doctor with the mask and the syringe. The voice of the doctor was familiar. The others were not. I could hear the familiar voice saying, we have to hurry. If this is going to work, we will have to use most of the eggs and sperm and keep her in the hospital for at least four days so I can make sure that it took. I jumped. This dream was more vivid than before. I was surer than ever before that Dr. Morgan performed the surgery, but she had help. I woke up Preston when I jumped. I reassured him that I was okay and settled back down as if to go to sleep, but that was the last thing I wanted to do. Eventually, exhaustion took over and I fell asleep.

The next morning Preston asked me if I had had a bad dream. I shared that I had had the dream again, but more detail this time. He shook his head as if to agree and asked me to write it down so that I could share it with the private investigator (PI) that he hired. I was surprised that he had a PI and forgot to share it with me. I ain't mad. In fact, I am quite pleased that he had taken charge of this process. I had almost forgotten that I had asked Alondra to find one for me. I should have known that my husband knew someone. After all, he is an attorney. Even though he is a corporate lawyer, they all know each other in some type of capacity. What was taking Alondra so long to find a PI anyhow? This situation is crucial. Preston shared that his detective would be flying out to Aspen by week's end and he was praying that he would find the answers that we needed. Our first instinct was to get a paternity test on Madison and then we thought better of it. She was a doctor who was desperate to get their baby. If she could convince a hospital in Aspen to lie about knowing her, there is no telling how far she would go.

Chapter 19

I am Travis DeWitt. I was hired by Preston Stone to find out what happened to his wife when they were in Aspen on their honeymoon. I arrived in Aspen on the morning of December 3rd. I love being in Colorado this time of year. This is an assignment I am going to make the best of for other reasons as well. The first thing I had to do was figure out how to get admitted to the hospital without causing suspicion. I have a sister in the Aspen area, but I have not seen nor talked to her in a long time. The last time I saw her, I was in a fist fight with her now ex-husband. I found out that Lisa's fiancé was unfaithful. I was trying to prove it before they got married because I knew she would not want to believe me once they were married. When I finally had the proof I needed, it was an hour before she was about to get married. She became angry, Derek and I got into a fight and she stated that she would never speak to me again. Whenever she came home and I was there, she refused to speak to me. In fact, she avoided me like the plague. She soon discovered that Derek was being unfaithful. She stayed for another year to give him a chance to do right by her, but he didn't. Finally, when he became so overt with his adultery, she had to be done with him or go to the penitentiary. Since she had already given up enough for this man, she wasn't willing to give up her freedom.

    I was hoping that I would get a chance to see her, but I knew my chances were slim that she would agree to see me. I have always known where she lived and I have her telephone number, but I wouldn't dare call or go see her. I knew she was able to take care of herself, but as her big brother I felt that it was my job to take care of her.

Enough of that! I am going to go to the emergency room with the one thing that is the hardest to diagnosis, why my back hurts. I went to the emergency room and signed myself in at the reception desk. After waiting for almost three hours, I was triaged and taken to a room. There was a bad car accident with multiple injuries so things were moving very slowly. Once in a room, a nurse came in to ask additional questions. The nurse took the information and stated that since the shift was changing a different nurse would finish taking care of me. She left. Roughly 45 minutes later, the nurse came in. She had curly golden hair, and about was 5'4 ½ inches tall. She was so beautiful. I couldn't believe it. It was Lisa. She didn't recognize me immediately because she wasn't looking directly at me and the name I was using was an alias. When I was asked to undress and put on the gown with the opening in the back, she looked at me and realized I was her big brother Travis. She just stood there stunned. She couldn't believe that it was me. She looked at the chart and asked what was with the alias. I shared that I was working on a case and that I couldn't use my real name. "Oh, imagine that. You aren't telling the truth. Old habits die hard, huh?" Okay, this is where this is going. It turns out I was right and she's still mad at me. Wow! I can't believe this. I started to get angry, but instead I said, "I am happy that I got a chance to see you even if you aren't happy to see me. I love you. By the way, I am staying at the Holiday Inn in case you want to see me again." I left the gown on the bed and left. After all this time, she is still angry with me. All I was trying to do was protect her. I guess I could have gone about it in a different way, but how do you tell your sister that the man that she loves is a low-down, two-timing dog. That hurt me to even say it. I am a dude after all.

I found something to eat and went back to the hotel. I was just about to eat my burger and fries when there was a knock on the door. It was my sister. I was shocked. I wasn't sure what to expect considering what happened at the hospital. She asked if she could come in. She entered and appeared to be searching for words, so we made small talk. She said that I had left my wallet at the hospital and since my hotel was within walking distance of the hospital, she decided she would bring it to me on her break. She handed me the wallet. For an instant, I thought it was mine, until I sat down and felt mine in my rear pocket. Whatever, I am just glad she is here. She stayed only 5 minutes, but it was a start.

The next morning I just walked around town trying to re-familiarize myself with the area. It had been about 10 years since I have been here. After a day of sightseeing, I went back to the hospital. I used the excuse that I didn't have my insurance card with me the night before and I was still having problems with my back so I came back. After I was triaged, I was placed in a room within an hour. Lisa was on duty and came into the room. She appeared to be less hostile than she was the night before. She made light conversation and then asked if I would like to go to dinner. I was stunned, but I agreed. This should be good. I hope it is a restaurant that won't put us out when we started arguing. Either way, I will take it. She left the room. The doctor came in to examine me. I shared my symptoms and he started the exam. As we made small talk, I casually mentioned that I use to date a girl that was once a doctor at the hospital. The doctor smiled and said, "And you let her get away?" We both laughed. "Yeah, real smart, right? Her name was Celeste." The doctor paused momentarily. He then continued the exam but looked at me as if I had said the wrong thing. I must be on to something. I asked if she still worked there because I would love to see her. The doctor stopped all the small talk. He stated that maybe I had strained my back and would need muscle relaxers and he was gone. "Ding, ding, ding, ding, ding! Travis you have got yourself a winner." I was given a prescription, a bill, and I was shown the way out. I had to figure out my next move. Nurses are usually the ones who know what's what; so I will have to get what I need from my sister. I just hope it doesn't take forever.

Chapter 20

Finally Celeste is out of the house and it was time for Mrs. Jones to find out what she was doing in her room with the door always closed. The room was in such disarray, she didn't know where to start. She was tempted to pick things up and put them in their proper place, but she was afraid that Celeste would know that she had been in there. Mrs. Jones had to be very careful about what she moved and how she moved it. This made the process take much longer than she anticipated. She wasn't sure what time Celeste would be back and she could not risk getting caught. As she scanned the room, she noticed something peering from under the pillow. As she was about to move toward it, she heard the door squeak. She turned and was about to scream when Mr. Jones grabbed her and covered her mouth. She jumped back and hit him on the arm and whispered, "What is wrong with you? I almost wet my pants! I thought you were Celeste!" He laughed out loudly. "There is no one here but us, but you need to hurry! I'll go and stand watch," said Mr. Jones.

He left the room and she moved toward the pillow. When she lifted it she was somewhat confused. She saw magazines for baby clothes, baby furniture, and the name of a child, Stephanie Celeste Morgan. "Who is Stephanie? Celeste can't have babies. Is she going to adopt?" She squealed with the anticipation of having a granddaughter. She put the papers back and was about to walk out of the room when she saw papers sticking out from under the bed. She thought to herself that there was no way in the world she could sleep in this mess. What she found next caused her heart to race. It was information about a surgical procedure she had performed on a woman named MacKenzie who would give birth to her and Steve's baby. As she read it she thought it was somewhat bizarre. She went on to describe what she would do after the baby or babies were born. She would pay MacKenzie an outrageous amount of money; move her practice from Seattle and move back into the home where she and Steve lived. Mrs. Jones was thinking that this should be good news, but her gut told her that there was something wrong. A whistle interrupted her thoughts. It was her husband. She had to go. She slid the information back under the bed and she left the room.

All afternoon she had to pretend that she had not seen the information in Celeste's room. She wanted to ask questions about what she had seen, but she couldn't without letting on to what she knew. She wasn't sure what she had read, but she knew something was not right. She had not shared it with her husband because she had not had time, but she couldn't wait.

The Joneses and Celeste enjoyed sitting in the family room watching television together. Celeste was in a light mood and appeared to be happier than she had been in a while. Mrs. Jones asked Celeste why she was in such a good mood. She asked where she had gone that afternoon since she was gone for the entire afternoon.

Celeste looked at her mom suspiciously. She turned her head slightly and asked, "Why do you ask? I wasn't gone that long. Were you worried?" Mrs. Jones stated that she was and that she had been concerned since she had been so upset and was staying in her room so much. She treaded lightly. Celeste chose her words carefully and said that she had visited with an attorney about some unfinished business concerning her and Steve. Steve passed away over two years ago and Mrs. Jones wondered what she could possibly have to see an attorney about. When she asked what she saw the attorney about, Celeste was evasive and never completely answered the question. "Well, the maid is coming tomorrow to clean the house. We have to be out by 9:00 a.m." Celeste looked stunned and said, "Under no circumstances is she to enter my room." Mrs. Jones said, "Baby, when the maid cleans the house, your room is included." She laughed. Celeste stated more assertively, "There is no way that she is to enter my room." Celeste got up and stormed out of the room much to her parents' surprise. Now, they both knew something was wrong.

Chapter 21

I wanted to know more about what happened. How was I able to deliver two children and one of them was not mine? I made an appointment to meet with a fertility specialist. Maybe this would make me feel better and be able to wrap my head around what happened.

I met with Dr. Benjamin Fortier. He was a well-known fertility specialist who could possibly help me complete the puzzle. When I made the appointment with the doctor I stated that I was interested in vitro fertilization, but needed additional information.

Dr. Fortier came in, shook my hand, and asked what I would like to know. He appears to be a nice, honest man; I feel convicted of my earlier plans. I shared with the doctor that I was not completely honest about why I needed to meet with him. He smiled as if intrigued. I shared my story about the delivery of my twins and that one was not my biological baby. "Please share with me how that could possibly happen." Dr. Fortier shared that while it could be possible for me to carry a child that is not my biological child and carry one that is at the same time, is extremely rare. While the impossible does happen, if eggs were implanted into your uterus at this time, you would have already been pregnant. That is why your doctor thought you had fraternal twins when in reality you were carrying two separate babies as a result of two separate actions. I was floored and confused. I couldn't believe what I heard. I could have been carrying someone else's baby. Dr. Morgan's baby. Why would she do it? There is no logical explanation for what she had done to me. I felt myself getting angry and tears beginning to form in my eyes. I suppressed them until I could leave the doctor's office and get to my car. After I was sitting safely in my car I started talking to the Lord. "Lord, I thought I was finished being hurt and angry. I am not sure why she chose me to have her baby, but I know that you do. I trust You and know that you will make this clear to me one day, but in the meantime, help me get through this because all I want to do is find Dr. Morgan and hurt her physically the way that she has hurt me, but I know that will only make things worse. Please don't let me find her until the right time so that I don't do something that I will regret." I started my car and headed home.

It was about 5:00 p.m. when I arrived home. This was a little early for me, but I wasn't able to go back to work after what Dr. Fortier and I discussed. I went in and saw the nanny feeding Madison. Madison squealed as usual when she saw her mommy. I smiled and went to my daughter to get my afternoon hug and wet baby kisses. The nanny completed her duties for the night and left at 6:00 p.m.

Preston was walking in as the nanny was leaving. He was home early tonight. That was good. I was happy to see him. "Hello my girls! Daddy's home! Who has kisses for daddy?" Maddie did her usual. A big toothless smile came across her face and she reached for Preston. Preston loved it! I stated very sarcastically, "I'm fine baby. I had a great day. How was yours?" Preston looked at me and smiled and said, "I asked who had kisses for daddy. You snoozed. Madison knows what's up." He continued to love on Madison as I walked by and pretended to hit him on the back of his head. He ignored me. The more Preston laughed and talked, the more Madison laughed and tried to talk back.

I went into the bathroom to get things ready for Maddie's bath. It was getting late and she would be going to bed soon. Preston brought his bubbly little one to me to begin our nightly routine. As I was laying Madison down for the night, I stood by her bed and stared at her. All at once, it hit me that it could have easily been Madison that had not survived the delivery. This shook me to my core. Before I knew it, I was thanking and praising the Lord that Madison had survived and that I had such a precious beautiful daughter to love. I realized how blessed I was and that I should be grateful for all that I had endured over the past months and that I was still standing and had my sanity by the grace of a loving God. I was so moved that I shed a few tears, but quickly recovered and joined my husband who had gone into the master bathroom to shower and get prepared for bed.

When he came out of the bathroom, I shared the contents of the meeting I had I with Dr. Fortier. Preston just shook his head in disbelief. I shared the thoughts that I had entertained in Madison's room. Preston shared that he had had the same thought before so he knew exactly how I felt. I smiled; we embraced, and shared each other's love before falling asleep for the night, wrapped in each other's arms.

Chapter 22

I was on time for dinner with Lisa. I was looking forward to this time with her no matter how it would turn out. We met at a steakhouse. A steakhouse has sharp steak knives…..I'm going anyway. Lisa looked as beautiful as she did on her wedding day. As I watched her, I had flashbacks of her as a little girl following me around asking a thousand questions and hanging on my every word. What I wouldn't do to relive those days. Lisa broke my train of thought when she was waving her hand in front of my face saying "Helloooo!" I snapped back to reality.

"Hey! Glad you made it." "I wasn't sure if I would come. There has been so much distance between us in the past three years that I wasn't sure how I would feel seeing you, or how you would feel about seeing me." "Are you kidding! I am just happy to be here with you even if it is to argue. I have missed you so much! I am sorry that things turned out the way they did. I never intended for things to happen the way they did." Lisa held up her hand to interrupt me and said, "It is me who should be sorry. I was stupid and angry because I knew you were right, but I couldn't face the truth, especially from you. I was embarrassed that I got played and……." By this time we were sitting in the same seat hugging as if nothing had ever separated us while people in the restaurant were looking at us like we had lost our minds. "Can you ever forgive me?" "What's to forgive?" We were at the restaurant for about three hours catching up on everything we could think of. We even reminisced about our childhood. After the restaurant we went back to her house and laughed until almost 2:00 in the morning. I had not felt this good since we had become estranged. Now that I was back in her life, nothing would ever change it again. Since it was so late, Lisa asked me to stay at her house. I could sleep in the guest room. She did not have to ask me twice. By 3:00 we were sound asleep.

Lisa didn't have to work the next day so we both slept in. We got up around 12:00 noon starving. We decided to cook whatever was in the kitchen for breakfast or lunch. As a nurse, she barely got a chance to go to the market. Pulling pots and pans, to cook, Lisa looked at me and asked why I was in town. She admitted that she knew I was a private investigator, and a good one at that. She knew that I was not in Aspen to see her so he must be working on a case. I shared Preston and MacKenzie's story with her. I showed her a picture of MacKenzie and the woman who had impregnated her. Lisa looked at the pictures and recognized Dr. Morgan. I couldn't believe it. I was FINAL-LY about to catch a break.

I asked what she knew about Dr. Morgan. Lisa told me how Dr. Morgan had completed her residency at the hospital where she worked. When she graduated from college, she was offered a position there. She was very good and so driven that she was soon on the board of directors of the hospital. "So, if she wanted to make something go away, she could, right?" "Yes, she could. What do you need?" "I need to prove that Dr. Morgan was the one who performed the procedure on MacKenzie when she was here on her honeymoon in January of this year. Can you do it?" "I think I can. There is always a paper trail." "Okay, how can I get access to the information?" "It will cause suspicion if I go to the hospital on my day off. Nobody does that, at least not a nurse. I will check on the first day that I return to work. I go back in three days. I work four days on, and three days off. In the meantime, you need to check out of your hotel and stay with me until your business is concluded." "Sure, I will do just that. Thank you Lisa. Have I told you that I love you and that I am glad we are spending this time together?" "Back at you big brother!" I left for the hotel.

Chapter 23

We met with our attorney at his office to prepare for what would happen next in the paternity suit filed by Dr. Morgan. He explained that in order for Dr. Morgan to gain custody of their daughter she would have to prove that Madison was indeed her daughter and that we entered into an agreement to give birth to her child and then willfully backed out of the arrangement. We figured that this should be easy to prove since no such thing happened. The attorney explained that Dr. Morgan's attorney has not agreed to meet with them at this point, but that nothing would transpire without them appearing before a judge to discuss the claim and present the evidence. He stated that we shouldn't worry and that he would try getting on the judge's docket so that we could bring this ordeal to a close. The meeting was over.

Here we are approaching the Christmas holidays which should be the most joyous time since it's our first Christmas as husband and wife and with our daughter Madison. Even though we were told that Preston II was not ours, I know in my heart that he was and I missed him dearly. Those few moments with him had a lifetime effect. It's hard to find joy in the midst of sorry, but I know I can. I have to. I have so much to be thankful for and I refuse to allow sadness and anger to overtake me. The fact that we are fighting for custody of our child is definitely threatening my peace and happiness, but I trust the Lord to make it right. I can't and won't give up hope for our happily ever after.

After the meeting I thought that we would be heading home, but Preston had other plans. Since it has been months since we had been on a date, Preston decided that we needed to go out for dinner and a movie. I agreed. It had been too long since we had had a chance to go out and enjoy ourselves and focus on just us. I was looking forward to it. I didn't know what movie we would see or where we would have dinner, but I didn't care. Madison was in good hands and I was going to enjoy myself.

Preston pulled up to a Mexican restaurant. Mexican is my favorite food so he knew he would earn points with this gesture. We had a cozy little seat in the back. We sat in a booth dimly lit by candlelight. This was going to be good. I looked forward to it. Preston was grinning from ear to ear. He was happy to see me relaxed and having fun. He thought I was the most beautiful creature he had ever seen in his life. Not because of my physical appearance, but for who I was inwardly. Hey, this is what he told me! I'm not mad. He thought I was sweet, kind, thoughtful, supportive, and one of the strongest women he knew. I reminded him of his mother and Grandma Edda. It was my spirit that he said drew him to me and that same spirit is what kept him loving me more and more each day. I didn't notice Preston staring at me. I was too busy deciding what I wanted for dinner. The server came to our table to take our order. I ordered the chicken fajita quesadilla, hold the guacamole, sour cream, and pico de gallo, and add extra lettuce. Preston ordered the house special. We ordered drinks and were relaxing when Preston's cell phone went off. I was a little annoyed, but decided not to make a stink about it. By Preston's responses I knew that it was not business. I sat anxiously until he hung up to ask what was going on.

He told me that his private investigator had finally gotten a break and that he should have answers for us in a few days. He stated that he finally believed that this nightmare was about to be over. We both smiled with excitement. We were sitting on separate sides of the booth, but after that good news we decided that they needed to sit a little closer. We needed to touch. The excitement was almost overwhelming. I wasn't sure what he would find, but I was hopeful that it would be what we needed. Preston prayed that it would be what we needed too.

The food arrived and we ate as if we had stolen it and was about to get caught so we had to hurry up. We ate with such enthusiasm; we hadn't eaten like this in awhile. It was a great day. After dinner we headed to the movies. I wanted to see a chick flick of course, but Preston wasn't having it. He wanted to see a movie with action. So we decided to compromise, if you can call it a compromise. We saw the new Transformers movie. I liked science fiction so it was okay. We had a great time, but it was time to go home. I was exhausted, but in a good way.

Thanksgiving Day was wonderful. We were excited to have family and friends over to celebrate our first Thanksgiving together. With all that we were going through seeing family and friends was going to be great. We were hosting dinner at our house. Our guests were expected to arrive at 2:00 p.m. for dinner. Everyone was bringing a covered dish. They were bringing their specialty. I was looking forward to it.

Everyone arrived promptly at 2:00 p.m. They must be hungry. I opened the door and everyone came in. I was so excited to see them. My parents and sisters were here and so was Mrs. Kingsley. Lorna and Khalil planned to come by later after they had dinner with her folks. The only person missing was Alondra. She stated that she wouldn't make it because she and Sebastian were going to visit her family for the holiday. She has been scarce these last few days, but I guess with everything going on I haven't been easily accessible. After everyone shed their coats they all sang out, where is Madison? It was so cute. This is what I am talking about. Some good people, some good food, and good times, I am definitely down with that.

It is December 1st. Time is moving so quickly. Madison is almost three months old. We have just celebrated our Thanksgiving together as a family and Christmas is right around the corner. I try not to concentrate on the negative things going on in regard to Madison's paternity. I am trying to enjoy myself and get prepared for Christmas. This will be our first Christmas together as husband and wife, and as a family. Wow! It is going to be incredible. We have to find a tree and decorate it. We have to decorate the inside and outside of the house. I have to shop for my family and friends. I have to prepare for me and Preston's first anniversary. How in the world will I get all of that done and go to work at the same time? I had to laugh to myself. It's all good. It will happen. No need to worry.

I can't believe it. It is Christmas Eve. The house looks great. My mom, dad, and sisters won't be coming to our house for the holidays and we wouldn't be going to theirs. Preston wanted me and Madison all to himself. I missed my family, but I am happy they came for Thanksgiving. This time of year was special for us. December 30th is what started our life together. I had wondered what our life would be like at one year. I have to say that it is not at all as I had imagined, but I am very happy.

Preston couldn't wait for us to exchange gifts. He was like a little kid who had just awakened to find that Santa had come and gone and left him everything he wanted for Christmas. We enjoyed watching Madison tearing at paper. At four months old, she was fascinated with the lights on the tree and all the colorful wrapping paper. We tried not to buy a lot of things for her because she was so young. We decided to start a tradition. Each year we would have a Christmas ornament with her name, picture and age on it to be added to the tree each year. Preston asked that I not buy him a gift because he had all he needed. It was a beautiful sentiment, but I bought him something anyway. He loves the Seattle Seahawks, so I gave him a NFL Seahawks leather athletic jacket. He was so excited. He put it on. He was beaming from ear to ear. Madison was sitting in my lap when he opened his gift. He handed me a box and reached for Madison. She held up her arms and cheerfully went to her daddy. I opened the box and found a beautiful gold locket with Madison on one side and baby Preston on the other. Preston made sure that he got a picture of baby Preston before he went to glory. I was in tears. It was the most thoughtful thing he had ever given me. I looked at him and he said, ever so sweetly as he fought back tears, "This is so you can kiss our babies whenever you feel the need." This is a Christmas that I will never forget.

It is December 30th and our one year anniversary. It is hard to believe that we have been married for one year. It feels like all we have had were hard times, I am so ready for some more good. I wished this custody fiasco was not hanging over our heads, but it is. I can't think about that right now. Oh my goodness! In all of the Christmas shopping, I didn't get Preston an anniversary gift. Okay girl, think. What in the world can I give him? I need to go to the store. Snap! The nanny is off until after the first of the year. Oh well, Miss Madison will have to go with me.

I went to the mall to purchase an anniversary gift. There were slim pickings for gifts. The first anniversary is paper. What in the word could I get that's paper? I looked around and then decided I would go make something. Then I saw it. A red Mrs. Claus suit that was going to make his eyes pop out of his head! Coupled with some red stilettos should do the trick. I was excited at the thought. I looked down at Madison as she was smiling up at me and I said "Don't look Madison. You are too young to see this." Madison and I headed home.

It was time for Madison's nap, so I laid her down and started my project. I am not artistic, but Preston would appreciate the thought. He's that kind of guy. I searched the website for ideas and decided upon a certificate. I created a certificate that read Mr. Preston Stone is entitled to one uninterrupted romantic night alone with his wife. He picks the place and the time. I printed it off, rolled it up, and sealed it with a kiss and tied it with a red ribbon. After a spray of perfume, his favorite scent, I was set. I called Mrs. Kingsley and asked if she could babysit tonight so that Preston and I could celebrate our anniversary. As it turns out, Preston had already requested her services. Sweet! She would be arriving at 5:00 p.m. I looked at the clock. It was 2:00 p.m. Come to think of it, where is Preston? He got up early this morning stating that he needed to go by the office and that he wouldn't be long and that I should not make plans for the evening. What is he up to? I'm sure I don't know, but I am sure it will be good. I smiled and decided I would take a nap so I would be fresh and rested for whatever the evening would hold.

Preston got home at about 3:30 p.m. He walked into the family room where I was sitting on the couch holding Madison. He was grinning from ear to ear. We were both up from our nap so Madison got her kiss and snuggle from her favorite man and so did I. He instructed me to get dressed in my sexiest red dress because we had dinner reservations at 5:30 p.m. Then he paused and said, "O yeah! You don't have a sexy red dress, do you?" "Uh, no" I said with a hint of sarcasm. "Go look in my closet to the left side." I jumped up and ran to the closet. I found a beautiful red dress. The left shoulder was out. The right shoulder and arm was covered by red lace. It was made of satin and covered in red sequins. It was breathtaking. There was a matching pair of red pumps covered in sequins to match. Well, alright now! Let's get this party started!!!! I ran to the bathroom to start getting dressed. He came in and told me to be sure and take my time he had Miss Madison occupied. I smiled and said "Yes sir!"

After an hour and a half I was ready to go. Mrs. Kingsley was there and loving on Madison when I walked in. I had not seen Preston since I went to my closet to get dressed. When he emerged, he was looking delicious. He looked at me and said "Wow!" When I saw him is all that I could say was "O my!"

We kissed Madison and headed out for the evening. We had a delicious dinner with live jazz playing in the background. For once in a long time all I could do was look at Preston… and want to get at him! Great day in the morning, this man is fine!!!!!!!!

After dinner, we went down by the bay. There was a yacht waiting to take us out for a cruise. A cruise? Does he know how cold it is out here? "Baby, you do know it's cold out here, right?" Preston responded, "I know. So you will just have to stay real close to me won't you?" I smiled and moved closer. We cruised around for about an hour sitting on the deck wrapped in a blanket. We also had hats, scarves, and hot chocolate on board. He had thought of everything. We had romantic music playing in the background. Then it happened. Jennifer Holiday's And I Am Tellin' You came on. I leaned forward and looked around at him and he was already laughing. I burst into laughter! We shared a passionate kiss as our cruise came to an end. This is the perfect ending to a perfect cruise.

We returned home about 11:00. I wondered where Mrs. Kingsley was. Preston shared that he had asked if she could stay all night. I was good with that. What would we do without Mrs. Kingsley?

We went upstairs to bedroom. I went in to take a shower so I could freshen up and warm up. Good grief it was cold, but it was so much fun. I would not have changed a thing. After a nice hot shower, Mrs. Claus made her appearance. Let's just say, Santa was very pleased. It was the perfect ending to a perfect day.

-155-

Chapter 24

Celeste continued to make preparations for her daughter to come home. She started to leave her parent's house more and more. She redecorated the house. She kept some personal things in the house that reminded her of Steven, but everything else had to go. She had a beautiful nursery in the house. It was a beautiful shade of pink with white accents. There were beautiful white butterflies on the wall flying toward the windows toward freedom. The bed had a beautiful white lace comforter that was one of a kind. Every time she went to the house and continued her work, she felt happier. Her parents noticed that her mood had changed and that she seemed happier. Her room at their house was also getting neater. She wasn't moody. Mrs. Jones was thinking that things were getting better.

Mrs. Jones decided that she would follow Celeste one day to see what she was doing with her time. Celeste said that she was preparing to move her office back home, but her mom wasn't convinced. Celeste left at her usual time. Since she didn't have a reason to be suspicious, she never noticed that her mom had followed her.

They rode for a couple of hours. She realized that she was going to the house that she shared with Steven. When Celeste pulled into the driveway, there was someone there waiting for her, a neatly dressed woman who appeared to be carrying a large notebook. They were inside for about 30 minutes when Celeste came out, got into her car, and left the house. Mrs. Jones took the opportunity to go inside and see what she could find out.

When she went into the house Jennifer, the interior designer, was there. Jennifer was startled because she thought she was in the house alone. "May I help you?" "Hi, I am Mrs. Jones, Celeste's mother. I came by to see how things were coming along." "Oh, I thought she was keeping it a secret until she was finished and Stephanie was home." "I guess the excitement over took her and she had to tell someone." "That's great! Let me show you the place." Mrs. Jones was escorted through the house guided by Jennifer. When they arrived at the nursery, there was a small pause to build the suspense. Then Jennifer pushed the doors open. The room was breathtaking. Mrs. Jones gasped as she saw the room. She couldn't believe how beautiful it was. Every detail of this room was well thought out and immaculately put together. Mrs. Jones was impressed. All of sudden Celeste walked in. Her mother had parked her car down the street so it could not be easily seen, so Celeste was wondering whom Jennifer could be talking to since no one else was supposed to be there. She walked in and saw Jennifer talking with her mom. She became unglued. Celeste started talking at the top of her voice. "What are you doing here? Who told you that you could come here? I don't remember inviting you? Get out!" Her mom and Jennifer were stunned by her reaction. Celeste repeated, "Get out!" "Celeste, baby…" "Shut up and get out, now!" Her mom retreated. She was out of breath when she arrived at her car. The tears were streaming down her face. Who in the world is that? Why had she responded so wildly? "Lord, what's wrong with my baby?" She drove away as quickly as she could.

Celeste fired Jennifer immediately after she ranted on incoherently for five minutes. Jennifer had no idea what had just happened, but she knew it was time to make her exit. She was about to leave with the plans for the remaining changes when Celeste snatched them out of her hands screaming that she bought them so they belonged to her. Jennifer didn't protest. She let go of them and exited the house as quickly as her four inch stilettos would carry her.

Celeste stood there as the room appeared to spin. Her plan was falling apart. How could her mom have known what she was doing? She had not told anyone what her plans were. She knew that she had to complete the renovations quickly before anything else went wrong. She looked around Stephanie's room and was pleased by what she saw. As long as this room was ready, she didn't care about anything else. She took her cell phone from her Prada bag that was hanging from her right arm and called her attorney. She simply stated, "It's time." She didn't wait for a response. She ended the call and went through the house to see what else she had to do before Stephanie came home. As far as she was concerned, she was done. She made sure all the doors were locked. She set the alarm and exited the house. Now, she had to deal with her mother.

Chapter 25

Finally Lisa returned to work. She reported to the emergency room as usual and began her workday. She knew today would be different. She felt it in her very soul that something big would happen. She and her brother had reconciled, she was happy, and she wanted to help her brother in any way she could. Since everything happened in the emergency room, it would be easy for her to move around to get what she needed.

Travis would have to wait at her house until she called. That was going to be hard, but he agreed to stay put.

After Lisa saw her first patient, as luck would have it, she was asked to access records on a patient that came in on or about January 2nd, a year ago. Her heart started racing. "Which record am I looking for?" "It was a patient that had surgery performed by a doc that may not have been on staff. It is being requested by some attorney." You have got to be kidding me. "Am I authorized to do that?" asked Lisa. "Yes, the person who used to do it before got fired because she was making too many errors. As it turns out, there was a failsafe on the records. It saves every three to five minutes no matter what. We could go back and look at the records prior to her making changes because she could never do them all at the same time." As casually as she could, she responded, "Oh." And she was gone. She tried calling Travis back at the house, but her hands were shaking so badly, she miss-dialed the number the first time. She reached him on the second try. "Travis, listen I don't have much time. I am about to access the record you were talking about. I will have the information you need this afternoon when I get home." She hung up. My heart was beating so loudly I thought I was having a heart attack. I took deep breathes to calm myself down. I had about ten hours to kill before Lisa would be home. She couldn't get home soon enough.

Lisa did as she was asked. She accessed MacKenzie's records. She made a copy of them for the attorney. While she was doing that, Travis telephoned Preston and stated that he needed MacKenzie to request a copy of her medical records immediately because another attorney was requesting them. If they didn't get a copy today, they could be altered and they would never be able to prove anything. He stated that he understood. The call ended.

By this time, Lisa had made the copy of the record and placed it on a CD. As she was preparing to close the record, she got the order to copy it again for a different attorney. She was trying hard to contain her excitement. She had no idea where all of this was going, but she knew this was something that would help Travis. She made the second CD and took them both to the mailroom to be mailed, but she also made a third copy for her brother. She couldn't wait to get home.

Once she arrived, we pulled up the CD and started reading it for anything that would stand out. Good thing Lisa had a computer so we could look at the CD. We saw the names of the nurses assisting, the anesthesiologist, and the doctor. What do you know? The doctor's signature is not legible. One of the nurses was none other than Lucy; the nurse who made all of the errors. I looked at Lisa and asked if she knew where Lucy lived. Maybe she could shed some light on what happened. Her smile meant yes. We ran for the door and headed to Lucy's.

It took us about 20 minutes to get to Lucy's house. When we arrived it was dusk and Lucy was heading into the house when we pulled up. She turned to see who was there. She recognized Lisa and smiled. "Hey stranger, how are you?" "I've been good Lisa. What are you doing in these parts of the woods?" "This is my brother Travis. He is visiting for a while. I will be honest with you; he is a private investigator working on a case. Do you think it would be okay to ask you a few questions?" "Sure, but I don't know how I could help." "Do you remember the surgery Dr. Morgan performed on January 2nd of last year?" "Yes, I do. Why?" We looked at one another. "Tell us what happened." "Well, the team was preparing for what we thought was an appendectomy when Dr. Morgan stated that that patient was being handled by another surgeon, this patient was here for in-vitro fertilization. We all looked at each other like...okay. Out comes the dish with the egg and sperm ready for transfer to the uterus. She performs the procedure and we think that we are done, when she makes a small incision in her naval area and perform another procedure. I have no idea why she did this because the procedure she needed to perform was done, but we didn't question it. After all, she was the doctor and should know what she was doing. After that, we sent the patient to recovery, Dr. Morgan scrubbed out and we were done. Why? Is she in some kind of trouble?" "We're not sure, but the patient she operated on is asking a lot of questions. We just wanted to know what happened." "Okay. I hope I helped." "Yes, you did. Thank you so much." "Hey, I am thinking about applying for a nursing job for Dr. Bennett, any chance I could get a reference?" "You got it!"

I didn't sleep much the night before. Lisa and I stayed up for hours talking again. I knew it was time to go home. I hated that I found the information I needed so quickly. I was enjoying the time I was spending with Lisa and I all I wanted to do was stay a few more days, but I knew how important it was for me to get back to Seattle with the information I had. I got up early the next morning and started packing. As I was packing to go home, I felt sadness. I had not spoken with Lisa in three years and now it had to come to an end. I left the guest room and headed to the kitchen where Lisa was waiting to say goodbye. She had been doing something for the last hour, but I didn't want to disturb her because I knew that our saying goodbye would be hard. Something smelled good. I grabbed my bag, took a deep breath and headed into the kitchen.

"Girl, what are you doing?" She turned around and said "Surprise!" She had made me my favorite thing, chocolate chip cookies. "Wow, chocolate chip cookies." No, she didn't. The last time this girl made chocolate cookies, I could use them as a weapon. How do I say no when we have had such an amazing visit. Lisa burst into laughter. "Boy, the last time I made you cookies, I was ten. I have gotten a lot better at it. Don't be scared." I laughed and took a cookie. Man these cookies are so good; they make me want to slap my grandmamma! My sister can finally make cookies. We both laughed and embraced.

"I have to go now" as I reluctantly let go of her. "I know" she said. "I love you." "I love you too. See you at Easter?" she asked. "You got it baby girl." We hugged once more. As we were hugging, I grabbed the rest of the cookies and ran. Lisa squealed the same way she did when they were little. What a sweet sound.

Chapter 26

Mrs. Jones was finally home. She was so shaken she could barely get out of the car. She took a deep breath, got out of the car and went into the house. She must have driven there on complete autopilot because she didn't remember driving; only arriving.

Mr. Jones wasn't home so she had more time to compose herself before he got there. She would need her energy to tell her husband what happened. There was nothing unusual about her wanting to move back into her and Steve's home, but everything about Stephanie didn't make sense. Where is she now? Why did Celeste respond the way she did about her being at the house? So many questions, but no answers. She heard the door open and close and thought it was her husband. It wasn't. It was Celeste. Her eyes looked wild and she was still very angry. Mrs. Jones wasn't sure what to expect at this point, but she was expecting a fight. She wasn't disappointed.

"Why are you following me around? You have no right to follow me! What I do is my business! Do you understand? Stay out of my life! I bet you have been in my bedroom too, haven't you? Answer me!" Celeste was screaming at the top of her voice. That is something that she has never done to either of her parents. Before Mrs. Jones could answer, Celeste began to cry hysterically. The parental instinct is strong no matter the situation. Mrs. Jones moved in to hold her and she became stiff as a board and started to back away. "What's wrong, baby? Celeste, please

talk to me. I love you. No matter what it is, it will be okay."
"Just stay away" she replied in a voice that was cold and distant.
Celeste went to her room and slammed the door.

On the heels of her slamming the door, Mr. Jones walked
in. "What in the world is going on in here? I could hear you two
outside." Mrs. Jones just collapsed in his arms and sobbed. He
held her close and tried to console her.

After about 30 minutes, he went in to check on Celeste.
She was sitting in the dark holding her pillow. Mr. Jones called
her name, but she didn't respond. He called her name again, still
no response. He turned on the light. She didn't respond. He
approached her and sat on the bed beside her. He touched her
arm. She turned her head ever so slightly, but she had no expression. He rubbed her hand and spoke to her in a low quiet voice.
He stated that she was going to be alright. Tears rolled down her
checks, but she said nothing. She turned her head back in its
original position and she just rocked.

Mr. Jones called for his wife and stated that they needed
to take Celeste to the hospital. Mr. Jones held her hand and led
her to the car. Celeste moved, but didn't appear to be conscious
of her movements. She said absolutely nothing. Her stare was
empty. Mrs. Jones drove as Mr. Jones sat in the back seat with
Celeste. Mrs. Jones was not taking any chances going anywhere
near Celeste with what had transpired earlier that day. Besides,
her dad has always had a way with her. She was very happy that
his charm still worked.

They arrived at the hospital and requested that Celeste be evaluat-
ed. She was admitted to the hospital for exhaustion. Her parents imagined
that hospitals are careful not to label anyone as having a mental melt down,
especially if they are a physician. After all she was the hometown girl who
had made it big. Celeste was about to get the help that she needed.

Chapter 27

I had returned to Seattle. I was happy to be home. I arranged to meet with Preston and MacKenzie the next day to fill them in on what I had discovered while in Aspen. I met with them at their home to share the incredible story that the nurse had shared with Lisa and me.

MacKenzie now knew why she kept having the dream about the lady in the mask. She now knows without a doubt that Dr. Morgan implanted the eggs, but she still didn't know why. They came to the conclusion that they may never know and that it would have to be okay, but they would do what they had to do to protect Madison from Dr. Morgan. If she thinks she is getting Madison she has lost her mind. MacKenzie and Preston asked that I meet with their attorney to report what the nurse had disclosed. I reassured that I would. The meeting ended.

Preston and I just sat there stunned. This story just keeps getting more and more incredible. "I would not believe this story, if I were not living it. At least we now have proof that Dr. Morgan is behind all of this and we can end this stupid custody battle. We embraced. The telephone rang. It was Alondra. We had not spoken in a few weeks and we desperately needed to catch up. I was happy to hear my friend's voice.

"Girl, what have you been up to? Did you ever find an investigator to help you with your case?" "Yes, he just left our house today. He found a nurse that was there during my procedure. This nightmare is about over. What have you been up to?" I asked. "Being in love and working hard. Glad this ordeal is about over for you guys. We need to hang out soon. We are way overdue" said Alondra. "Yes, we are! I love you friend." "I love you too. Please keep me up to date on what's happening. Okay?" said Alondra. "Sure, will do" I responded. The call ended. I went in to check on Madison who was down for a nap. My sweet angel was sleeping so peacefully. I left her room and went to find Preston. He was on the couch watching television; or rather the television was watching him. He had fallen asleep. Her guardian angel was asleep. He was cute, sleeping peacefully, but he was snoring like a pig. There is no way I am staying in there with all that noise. Since it was the weekend, I decided that I would do absolutely nothing. It feels good to do nothing. Every mom needs a time when she can do nothing, but rest and I am going to do my best to make it happen. Just as I lay down, Madison sang out. I had to laugh to myself. Well, at least the thought should count for something. I must have been on the telephone longer than I thought.

Chapter 28

Celeste was transferred to a mental health facility. After being there for three days, she was allowed to have visitors. When she saw her mom and dad, she was very happy. She ran and embraced them both. After a few moments, they sat on a couch to talk. She was once again the little girl, insecure and vulnerable who very much needed her parents.

They started with the usual how are you and then the awkward silence. Celeste bore her soul to her parents. She told them about her and Steve's difficulty with conceiving and after her miscarriage. How she put large amounts of concentrated antihistamines in MacKenzie's hot chocolate to make her sick so she could implant her fertilized eggs into her uterus so she could deliver her and Steve's baby. She cried as she told the story. Her parents cried and held her hand. "She was the perfect candidate. MacKenzie is smart, in excellent physical condition, and she had just gotten married. It was perfect. I had not completely thought out my plan because it never occurred to me that one of the babies would die or how I would convince her to give me my babies. I couldn't let just anyone carry my babies. It had to be her. MacKenzie and her husband have my baby, and I want her. I need her. Stephanie is all I have left of Steve. Please tell me you will help me get her from MacKenzie. I don't think I could survive without her." Her parents sat and looked at her in complete horror. Celeste had become so distraught that the doctor ordered a sedative and put Celeste to bed. Her parents stayed with her until she was completely asleep. Mr. and Mrs. Jones met with Celeste's doctor. Dr. Fredericks was the attending psychiatrist. He shared that Celeste was in need of rest and that she was having a psychotic episode due to trauma and stress. He wasn't sure how long she would have to be there, but he would keep them updated on her progress. After listening careful, The Joneses thanked him for his time and then they headed home.

Mrs. Jones cried all the way home. She couldn't help it. Her daughter was hurting and she needed to help her, but she didn't know how. They had no idea how long Celeste would be in the hospital or how much of her bizarre story was true. This was way too much information for them to process. Time heals all wounds. Celeste needed a lot of time for her wounds ran deep.

Once they arrived home, they went in to have a snack and rest as they figured out what to do next. One thing they would do is try to figure out the name of the attorney that Celeste had retained to see if he could shed some light on what was going on. They hoped they would find the information they needed in Celeste's room since she had not removed all the things from her room.

Mrs. Jones started on one side and Mr. Jones started on the other. Mrs. Jones started with the pillow. Nothing. She looked under the bed. Nothing. Mr. Jones looked in the chest of drawers and the dresser and he was unsuccessful as well. Mrs. Jones moved to the closet. Bingo! Celeste had a neat little file with all of her information categorized and alphabetized. Mrs. Jones found information about Celeste's attorney, Mr. Lawrence Thompson. He would be where they started, but not today. They had all they could handle for one day. The information that she saw earlier concerning Stephanie was not there, but she was sure the attorney would be able to help them with that as well.

Chapter 29

$\mathbf{M}$r. and Mrs. Jones were up early on Monday morning to meet with Mr. Thompson concerning Celeste's case. Mr. Thompson stated that he couldn't discuss anything with them as they were not authorized to receive any information. Mrs. Jones pleaded for the information, but he refused stating attorney – client privilege. They thanked him for his time and left his office. Mrs. Jones stated that she would get the clearance that they needed. Mr. Jones asked how she proposed to do that. She answered that Celeste would give it to them. He wasn't sure that Celeste was in the right frame of mind to give them permission. On the contrary, this is the right time to get the permissions they needed.

When they returned home, Mrs. Jones telephoned the facility where Celeste was receiving help. She left a message for Dr. Fredericks to contact them about Celeste. They would not be allowed to visit her again for a week and Mrs. Jones felt as if they were running out of time.

Mr. Fredericks returned Mrs. Jones call later that evening after he had visited all of his patients. Mrs. Jones stated what she needed and why. She asked if he could obtain permission for Celeste for them to move forward with whatever she was working on. He stated that at this time she was not competent enough to do that, but they could petition the court for power of attorney to act on her behalf during her illness. She thanked him for the information and the call ended. They hated to have to go this route, but they had to do what they had to do to help Celeste through this horrible time in her life. At least, until she was better. Mr. Jones agreed that they should move forward. They would obtain the necessary documents from Dr. Fredericks and petition the courts. They had no idea how long it would take or how much it would cost, but they would move forward first thing tomorrow morning.

The Joneses arrived at the clerk's office of the Probate Court on Tuesday morning asking to be given the power of attorney for their daughter who was in a hospital and who was temporarily unable to make decisions for herself. The clerk provided them with a list of what they needed. They would have to obtain information from her doctor and sign the documents in the presence of a notary public and file it with the courts. Whew! That is a lot to do, but it is necessary to help Celeste in her efforts to get Stephanie back.

Now, before any of this can happen, Mrs. Jones felt it only fair to talk with Celeste about their plans and see if she would consent to her mother speaking with the attorney. If she did, all of these steps would be unnecessary. The only thing is that she would not be able to see Celeste for another week and she didn't want to wait so long. She was anxious to find out what was really going on in her daughter's life. She had not really had any friends since medical school. She has worked so hard and was always so focused on being a successful doctor. All she ever wanted to do was to become a doctor, marry Steve, and have a family. All of that appears to have slipped away. That has to be why she is having such an emotional break. Every time Mrs. Jones thought about what she had learned, it made her more anxious to learn more, but she was going to have to be patient. It has taken this long, she could wait another week, she hoped.

Mrs. Jones continued to go through Celeste's things to

find any clues she may have left behind. She had looked at the papers in the organizer for the 100th time, but felt she had missed something. She continued to comb through the papers again ever so slowly until she found the court papers. Bingo! She was thinking how in the world could she have missed it, but it is easy to miss what is right in front of you when you are unsure of what you are looking for. She wasn't sure that she would understand everything that was in the document, but she was going to try. And if she could not figure it out, she would find an attorney of her own to help it make sense.

From what she had read so far, she was accusing some woman named MacKenzie of giving birth to her babies and refusing to give Stephanie to her. Then there was a lot of jargon that she couldn't make out, so she gave up. She felt as if she had enough information to proceed. Then it came to her, forget the attorneys and all the other foolishness. She was going right to the source, MacKenzie. She was trying to remember if Celeste had mentioned where MacKenzie lived during her mumbling. She looked at the court document and there it was, the city and state where the motion was filed, Seattle, Washington. She knew her last name was Stone. How many MacKenzie Stone's could there be in Seattle?

Mrs. Jones got on the Internet and googled MacKenzie Stone. She saw a listing for MacKenzie Clay. She wondered if that was her. She doesn't have the same name, but it was worth a try. It was actually the telephone number for Loving Hearts. Hmmm, she is a psychiatrist? Wow! That's a hoot, she thought. A psychiatrist losing her mind and trying to keep someone else's child; if this is even her. Mrs. Jones looked at the clock. It was 5:30 p.m. on a Friday afternoon. "Well, no one in their right mind is at work on Friday at 5:30 if they can help it." She sighed. "I guess I will have to wait until Monday." She placed the items in a neat stack on the bed and decided it was time to find Mr. Jones so they could eat and settle for the evening.

Just as she was about to call out for Mr. Jones, the telephone rang. "Hello." "Mom, how are you?" "I'm fine. What's wrong?" "Nothing. I wanted to see you tomorrow if possible." "Sure. Will you be able to come" "Sure, dad and I will be there. What time can we come?" Mrs. Jones asked. "Visitation starts at 1:00 p.m." replied Celeste. "Okay, we will be there." The call ended. "Oomph, talk about timing?"

Chapter 30

The Joneses arrived promptly at 1:00 p.m. They were anxious to see Celeste. When they were there six days ago, she was not doing well at all. They had hoped that this visit would be different.

Celeste had invited her parents to attend a family session with her. They met with Dr. Fredericks. Celeste appeared very nervous about the session. Her parents could sense her anxiety and was ready to get the meeting started as well. Celeste stated that there were things that she wanted to share with them. She thanked Dr. Fredericks for how well she was now feeling even though she knew she still had a lot of recovery ahead of her. Now that she had had some rest and medication she was beginning to deal with her issues. She was feeling stronger and more stable and needed to be free of her demons. Her parents listened very intently. Celeste shared that she had not told her parents about everything that happened with MacKenzie. She confessed that MacKenzie was not a willing participate in her pregnancy. All she knew is that she saw the opportunity to have a child with Steve and nothing else mattered.

"MacKenzie was a patient of mine before she got married. At the time when she came to see me, she was not planning to get married any time soon. At her initial visit I asked if she was planning to have children. She said that she needed a husband first. I told her that there was another way to conceive a child without having a husband. I gave her the information about in vitro fertilization. She just smiled, but she kept the information. I thought she may be the one that I was looking for, but she became engaged within six months. She was getting married to a handsome attorney on New Year's Day and going to Aspen for her honeymoon. I know because we have a mutual friend, Alondra. Alondra told me about her plans to get married, but thought that I should speak with her about possibly being a surrogate for me. I shared with Alondra that she didn't appear all that interested when I mentioned in vitro fertilization to her. Alondra told me that it wouldn't hurt to ask her and that she would speak with her about it as well. I figured she would never agree to give birth to my children so I made the decision to impregnate her with my fertilized eggs. Since I had completed my residency and had worked at the hospital in Aspen, I had no problems setting things into motion. I am still on the board of directors and still have surgical privileges there. I called the lab where my eggs were being kept in Seattle and I had them flown to Aspen. I didn't have much time to make my move so I went to Aspen a week ahead of them. I checked into the lodge where they would be staying and I waited. Preston and MacKenzie arrived on January 2nd. I knew it was just a matter of time until I saw them so I had to be ready. I put something in her hot chocolate. I knew that she would become ill in a matter of hours, so I waited in the lobby for her to be taken to the hospital where my plan would go into action. I implanted the eggs, made sure she stayed in the hospital for a few days and then I flew home. They both came into my office six weeks later. I confirmed that she was pregnant. I took excellent care of her. She did her job by eating right and keeping all of the appointments. I was so excited when I discovered that she was pregnant with twins. And then it all fell apart. Women with multiple births deliver early, but I never expected there to be a complication. MacKenzie must have done something wrong. She is the reason my son died and now she has my daughter and I want her. I don't care how it happens, I want my daughter." The doctor and the Joneses sat there stunned. They knew for certain now that Celeste was mentally unstable. Before she could get over losing Steve, she thought she lost her children and it sent her into a downward spiral.

"My daughter is out there with MacKenzie and her husband. I know what I did was wrong. I am truly sorry for what I have put them through, but when I am well enough to leave this facility, I want my daughter home with me. Can you understand that?" "Yes, we can," answered her mom softly. We would like to help you. We went to see your attorney, but he refused to discuss anything with us without your consent" explained her mom. "I'll take care of that Monday morning. Please expect a call from Mr. Thompson on Monday afternoon to arrange a time to meet. I welcome your help. I should have told you this long time ago. I don't know what the consequences of this will be, but it will be worth it if I can get my daughter." The doctor shared that she was not a threat to herself or anyone else, so she could be released on Monday if she wanted to be released, but she was definitely in need of further psychiatric help. The Joneses stated that they understood. Celeste beamed. She thought that this changed everything. She could proceed for herself, but she definitely wanted mom and dad by her side to help through what came next, whatever it was. Mr. and Mrs. Jones agreed to come and pick Celeste up on Monday. After all this time, they finally understood what happened. They were still in utter disbelief that she could have consciously committed such an act against another person, but they had to help her get her daughter. They were happy that their daughter was going to be coming home, but she was far from being alright. They hoped their granddaughter would be home soon and be a part of their lives even though Celeste's future was very uncertain. The session ended. They spent another couple of hours with Celeste before they headed home.

Neither of them said much on the ride home for the first 20 minutes. Mrs. Jones finally said, "Baby, I don't think this is going to turn out the way she thinks it will. She committed a crime. She will have to answer for that. But what if she doesn't get custody and worst of all, what if Stephanie isn't her child. Then what?" "Well, we can't think the worst. Let's just see how it plays out. Either way, I feel like we are a family again and we will help each other get through this" expressed Mr. Jones. "No matter what?" Mrs. Jones asked. "No matter what," Mr. Jones confirmed.

Monday arrived and Celeste was coming home. She insisted that they go straight to Mr. Thompson's office. She wanted to schedule a time to meet with MacKenzie and Preston before they went before a judge. Mr. Thompson was not in, but his assistant, Mrs. Pearl, stated that he would be in Tuesday morning. Celeste shared with Mrs. Pearl that she wanted a meeting with the Stones and their attorney as soon as possible. Mrs. Pearl stated that she would contact the Stones attorney and then contact her with a time and a place for the meeting. Celeste agreed that this would be fine. Celeste and her parents headed home so that she could get home and settled. She had always felt at peace when she was home with her parents. She'd hoped that this time she would get the peacefulness she needed. She was ready to have peace and move on with her life.

By the time the Joneses were home and settled, Mrs. Pearl called. She informed Celeste that she had spoken with MacKenzie and Preston's attorney. The Stones agreed to meet the next Wednesday at 8:00 a.m. sharp at the office of the Stones attorney. Celeste was going back to Seattle to get Stephanie.

Chapter 31

It was 4:00 a.m. the day of the meeting and I couldn't sleep. All I could think of was meeting with Dr. Celeste Morgan. I didn't know how I would react, but I was ready to get it over with. I had called my parents, sisters, and my girlfriends to let them know that the meeting was finally happening. I asked them to pray that the truth would be revealed, that for once and for all that the custody issue would be resolved, and to pray any other way that they were led to pray.

Preston woke up to find me sitting in Madison's room staring at her and stroking her hair through the rails of the crib. Madison was now four months old. She is trying to crawl and pull up on everything she can get her little hands on. I kept thinking to myself about the events leading up to this day. Madison is the joy of our lives. For a brief moment, I was afraid that my baby would go away. I shared what I was thinking with Preston. He shared that he had entertained the thought, but he knew better. There was no way that Madison was going anywhere. I leaned my head back on Preston's chest for comfort. We remained at Madison's crib for a few moments more and then Preston put me back to bed. He snuggled beside me and we both went to sleep.

The alarm clock went off at 6:00 a.m. We got up and prepared for the day. I went to my closet to select something to wear. While I was in there, I said a prayer. It brought me the peace I needed. Preston was in his closet doing the same. He also had a peace that he had not experienced before. After we loved on Madison we left for the attorney's office. It was 7:15. It would only take us about 20 minutes to get there so we had plenty of time, but that would be a long 20 minute ride.

Celeste was up early as well. She and her parents had driven in from Denver Sunday night. She didn't sleep much last night because she was excited about today. All she could think of was bringing Stephanie home. She had hoped that Stephanie would be with MacKenzie and Preston, but she knew that this was only wishful thinking. She was up, dressed, and ready to go by 5:00 a.m. Her parents were not ready to go until 7:00 a.m. Dr. Morgan and the Joneses had agreed to meet at the Stones attorney's office at 7:30 a.m. Celeste didn't care where the meeting happened. She was just ready to get it over with.

We were all led into a large conference room. Each of us was given a set of instructions on how to conduct ourselves during the meeting. We were also given an idea of what to expect during the proceedings. Each party knew that this was the step before we all went before a judge. The Stones didn't look at Dr. Morgan nor Mr. and Mrs. Jones and Mr., and Mrs. Jones nor Dr. Morgan looked at the Stones.

Mr. Thompson, who represented Dr. Morgan, began his opening statement about how I was purposefully keeping a child from her mother because of the loss of the little boy that I thought was my son. He went on to say that while they sympathize with our loss, the truth is neither of the babies belonged to us; therefore, we are illegally keeping Dr. Morgan from her daughter. No charges would be pressed if we would immediately turn over custody of Baby girl Morgan to her mother, Dr. Celeste Morgan.

Our attorney, Mr. Lance, took a deep long breath, and

then went in for the kill, "Whose baby? Mr. Thompson if you had checked medical records more thoroughly, the original records, the unaltered documents; you would have remembered that each child is blood typed at birth. While it was stated that Preston II was not the son of the Stones, the test was not accurate. At the request of Mr. Stone, a genetic specialist completed a DNA profile on Preston, II, and Madison. With 99.9% accuracy, MacKenzie and Preston Stone are the biological parents of Madison Dianne Stone and Preston Stone, II. He handed Mr. Thompson the documents for his review. There was a mix up at the hospital and the blood type identified for baby boy Preston was wrong. How there was a mix up, I am not sure, but be assured that a full investigation will be conducted. I can assure you we will get to the source of the mix up. He went on to share that the records that were obtained from the hospital in Aspen proved that his client willfully and purposefully tried to impregnate his client without her consent. Then looking at Dr. Morgan, he continued. "In your quest to prove that you and your late husband Steve were the biological parents of the Stone twins, we received the report proving that it is impossible that either of you were the parents of the twins as your blood type is A+ and your husband's blood type was AB+". I looked at Preston. I couldn't believe it. Preston was our baby and Madison is our baby. He took care of it. He took care of me. He never said a word, but Preston was always in the background taking care of our babies and me. At that point I couldn't hear what the attorney was saying. It didn't matter. It was over for me.

Dr. Morgan just sat there in silence. She was motionless. It didn't work. All that planning, everything was perfect and it didn't work. She looked at Mr. Thompson and then to her parents. Her parents had tears in their eyes.

Our attorney, Mr. Lance began to speak again. We listened intently. Again looking at Mr. Thompson, Mr. Lance went on to ask "After Dr. Stone gave birth, what plan Dr. Morgan had for gaining custody of the child or children? Was she going to commit another unlawful act? Mr. Thompson your client is lucky that I do not have the police here right now to arrest her for her crime. We insist that the proceedings to gain custody of a child that does not belong to your client stop and desist immediately. We know that your client is in need of psychological help; however, in light of the situation, I still plan to press charges against her and go after her medical license. I have spoken with the district attorney and he has agreed to give Dr. Morgan two hours to turn herself in upon the conclusion of this meeting. We have taken the liberty of freezing her assets and accounts just in case she gets any ideas of taking any unscheduled vacations." Mr. Lance looked directly at Dr. Morgan and stated, "You did not abide by the Hippocratic Oath where it states to do no harm. You purposely caused harm to another human, not just physical, but emotional as well. One innocent baby died. What would have happened if all parties died; the mother and the babies?"

Mr. Thompson was about to speak when Dr. Morgan interrupted. She asked if she could speak. Dr. Morgan looked at us, with tears in her eyes, she started to speak. "I was so blinded by my grief and pain that I couldn't see what I was doing to myself, let alone what I was doing to the two of you. When I realized what I was doing, it was too late to back down. I had to go through with it. I need you to know what happened and what started all of this. I was married to the love of my life, my husband Steve. I was pregnant once and had a miscarriage. As fate would have it, I couldn't get pregnant, let alone carry a child because of my damaged uterus. Steve and I accepted that I couldn't give birth the way we thought the Lord intended so I would need a surrogate. A fertility specialist extracted my eggs and obtained a sperm specimen from Steve and we waited for the perfect person to come along to have our baby. He died in a car crash six months after the plans were made. As luck would have it, our mutual friend Alondra recommended you to me. When she mentioned you I remembered our conversation when you came to for your first office visit and I gave you the in-vitro fertilization brochure to read as an alternative to having children without being married. You never said you weren't interested or opposed to the idea. From that point on, I knew I wanted you to be the surrogate, but I didn't know how to do it. When Alondra told me that you and Preston would honeymoon in Aspen, I knew that would be the only opportunity for me to impregnate you because that is where I started practicing and no one would be the wiser. I put a drug in your hot chocolate to make you sick so that you would have to go to the hospital. I even made an incision at your naval to make you think you had an appendectomy. You received special treatment from my office because I told them you were high risk because of age. The nurses wouldn't question me. When you developed preeclampsia and the babies had to come early, I still wasn't concerned until my son died. That's why I disappeared soon after that. I couldn't bare it. I had lost my son and didn't know how I would get my daughter…your daughter. I would understand if you hated me because of all the pain I have put you both through. I am going to voluntarily relinquish my medical license. What I did was unethical and illegal and I did the one thing that I swore not to do, that is to do no harm. I am so sorry. I will not bother you again. I will speak with my lawyer about compensating you for all the turmoil I have put you through. I am not a bad person, but I have done some horrible things that I must answer for and I will do them gladly."

Did she say Alondra recommended me? What does she mean recommended me? I never spoke with anyone about being a surrogate for anyone. Preston and I just looked at one another. I just thought to myself, I can't believe Alondra told her that I wanted to be a surrogate parent. No wonder she was dragging her feet with helping me find a private detective and has all but disappeared from my life when I have needed support the most. She's just as crazy as Dr. Morgan. I will deal with her later. You better believe it's on! Here Dr. Morgan is sitting here talking with our attorney and us about compensating us like she hit our car. That is the funniest thing I've ever heard. She's talking as if she has come to that decision on her own. LOL! O yeah! She is out of her mind!

Mr. and Mrs. Jones sat there listening in complete disbelief. While they did not approve of what Celeste had done, they had agreed to stick by their daughter and that is what they were going to do. Praying that one day, the Stones would forgive their daughter and that one day she could forgive herself.

We asked if it was okay for everyone except our attorney to step into the hallway. Everyone exited the room. I was still trying to process everything that had happened. The one thing that I wanted to do was to walk out of this room and jump on top of Dr. Morgan and beat her until I felt no pain, but I knew that was not the answer. It wouldn't change the events that had happened. It wouldn't stop our pain. I just looked toward the heavens and said, "Lord, I need your help. You know what I want to do, but I would rather do what you want me to do." I looked at Preston and said, "I know at some point, I will forgive her, but it won't be today. I am too angry and too hurt right now, can we just go home? I pray that she will be able to get the help that she needs, but if I see her again anytime soon I will not be responsible for what I might do." "You would have to get in line baby girl" Preston stated as a matter of fact. I looked at Preston and laughed. I fell into his arms as Mr. Lance looked on. Preston turned to him and said, "Thank you friend. We are done." I looked at Preston and asked, "Friend?" "Yes, you have forgotten that I am an attorney and a pretty good one at that. Mr. Lance is one of the attorneys I used to play golf with until our lives unraveled." "You play golf?" "Cute, real cute." Preston turned and looked at Mr. Lance and stated "Mr. Lance, you may invite them back in." We left his office using an alternate door."

When Dr. Celeste and the Joneses reentered the room, they were surprised when only Mr. Lance was present. Mr. Lance announced that the process was over. Mr. Thompson stated that he would withdraw the petition for custody immediately. Mr. Lance exited the room.

We headed home to Madison. On the way home, I called my mom and asked her to three way call my sisters. I let them know that all went well. I thanked them for their prayers and told them that we would be having a celebration soon. Spread the word.

After I hung up, I stated to Preston that I actually feel sorry for Dr. Morgan, but not enough not to go after her to make sure that she doesn't do this to anyone else. "What I can't believe is that Alondra set all this in motion. Was she ever truly my friend? Preston she smiled in my face and acted as if she was concerned about us when she never was. I don't know who I despise more, Alondra for being stupid enough to set this in motion or Dr. Morgan for participating." "Don't worry baby, I got this. You trust me?" "Yes sir. I do."

Things were finally settling down. I was happy and had returned to work. Preston had done the same. This ordeal taught us how to trust the Lord no matter what it looks like. I know in this midst of the storm when I am being tossed to and fro and can't seem to get my footing, that He is right there holding my hand.

Chapter 32

The next day after it all hit the fan; there was a knock at the door. I went to the door. "Alondra Venazuela?" "Yes." "You are under arrest for conspiracy to commit kidnapping. You have the right to remain silent. Anything you say can and will be used against you in a court of law. You have the right to talk with an attorney while you are being questioned. If you cannot afford to hire an attorney, one will be appointed to represent you before you are questioned if you wish. You can decide at any time to exercise these rights and not answer any questions or make any statements. Do you understand each of these rights that I have explained to you? Having these rights in mind, do you wish to talk to us now?" "No, I do not" I answered as a matter of fact. I need to call my attorney.

Me, Alondra Venazuela, arrested! I was placed in handcuffs and transported to the police station in the back of a squad car. Once we arrived at the police station, I was booked. They took me into a room where I was searched and all of my personal belongings were inventoried and placed in a bag with my name clearly displayed. I was then fingerprinted, and the most humiliating part of it all, was when I had to hold those numbers across my chest and take a picture. They asked me if I had any medical issues. Normally no, but right now, I am about to have a heart attack! I cannot believe that I have been arrested for conspiracy to commit kidnapping. What in the world are they talking about? Who was I conspiring with? Who are we trying to kidnap? I need to get out of here. After the picture was taken, I was taken to a cell where I had to wait to see a judge because I was being charged with a felony. I think the officer who put me in this disgusting cell stated that I have to wait 24 to 36 hours before I will go before a judge to plead guilty or innocent during my first appearance and that I could have an attorney present at that time. 24 to 36 hours before I can see a judge or go home. I was so terrified I was shaking. Here I am in this small cell for the entire world to see with a toilet looking at me. There is no way I am sitting on that. I have no idea why I am here. Oh no! MacKenzie! But how would she have known that I knew anything unless…….Celeste told her. I wonder if she told her the truth. I need to call Sebastian and get an attorney to get me out of here.

"Mom, dad, I am so sorry that I put you through this. I have no idea what happened. I have no explanation for what I did. Being in jail last night was humiliating and terrifying. What's worse is that I may have to go back to the hospital. I need to speak with Mr. Thompson about my options and what I should expect when I go before the judge again." "Celeste, as we stated before, we will be here for you no matter what, but you need help and we will make sure that you get what you need. You have made a mess and it is going to take a lot to clean it up, but it can be done. In the morning we are taking you back to the hospital so you can be admitted. We should have done this a long time ago; we didn't. We thought you had a handle on things. The truth is you don't. You will still have to face the medical board and the police, but for right now, you will get the psychiatric support you need. Now you can go voluntarily or I can call an ambulance, say that you are having a psychotic episode and have them pick you up and transport you. Which do you choose?" Celeste got angry. "Excuse me?" Celeste asked. "You heard me. I don't know who you are anymore. What you did was unspeakable and people who do these types of things need help. You are going to get that help if I have to get a court order. Understand? ""Yes ma'am" responded Celeste. Mrs. Jones walked into the kitchen to get something to drink when she noticed Mr. Jones standing next to the counter with a huge smile. "What are you smiling about?" she asked with a confused expression. He walked closer to her and stated that he was happy to see her being herself again. She smiled. He gave a smooch on the lips. It's late and time to rest for the night. Early the next morning, Mrs. Jones got up to check on Celeste and ask if she wanted breakfast before they left for the hospital. She knocked on the door. There was no answer. She knocked again, no response. She thought maybe she had gone to the bathroom. She knocked on the bathroom door. There was no answer. Mrs. Jones opened the door and saw that the bathroom was empty. She went back to Celeste's room and knocked again. When she didn't get an answer, she opened the door and went in. Celeste was gone. Mrs. Jones went to the front door to check for her car. Her car was not in the driveway. Mrs. Jones went to her bedroom to alert her husband. She told him that Celeste was gone. He was lying in bed. He sat up and asked his wife where she thought she may have gone. She stated that she wasn't sure. They just there and looked at one another. "We did all we could. She'll have to find her way back on her own" said Mr. Jones. "I know, but it still hurts" Mrs. Jones stated as she leaned on her husband and wept.

Chapter 33

Sebastian bailed me out of jail. I tried to explain to him what was happening, but I was just too upset. He stated that he would support me no matter what. We'll see. How dare that judge speak to me as if I were a criminal. I didn't do anything wrong and I am not going down for something I didn't do. I need to speak with Celeste, but my attorney has advised me that I should not have any contact with her at this time. She is the only one who can straighten out this mess and I can't have contact with her. Ugh! I need to call Mrs. Kingsley.

"Hello Mrs. Kingsley, this is Alondra." "How are you? Baby, are you alright? MacKenzie told me what happened." "What?" I exclaimed. "MacKenzie told me that you and Dr. Celeste Morgan were arrested for what happened to baby Preston. When was she arrested?" "She turned herself in on Wednesday after she met with Preston and MacKenzie at their attorney's office." "Mrs. Kingsley, I don't know what she told you, but I need you to understand what really happened. Is it okay if I come and see you? I really need a friend right now." "Sure, you can come by tomorrow at 6:00 p.m." "Okay, thank you Mrs. Kingsley." The call ended. Mrs. Kingsley had the bright idea of trying to get Alondra and MacKenzie together so that they could talk face to face with no one else present but her. She knows that both ladies love her and trust her so she hoped that she help them in this situation. MacKenzie was already coming by to see Mrs. Kingsley to give her a small token of her appreciation for all that she had done for her, Preston, and Miss Madison through the last six months, so this was perfect.

The next day MacKenzie arrived at Mrs. Kingsley's house at 5:30 p.m. She was stopping by on her way from work. "Hello Mrs. Kingsley, how are you? It's good to see you." "I am good. It is always good to see you. How is Miss Madison?" "She is great! Growing like a weed every day. I have something for you. It's a token our appreciation for all that you have done for us throughout this past year. You are the closest thing I have to family here. I don't know what we would have done without you. We love you very much!" Mrs. Kingsley smiled and opened her gift. It was a framed picture of Madison with a gift card to a major department store. She was happier with the picture than she was with the card of course. She got up and placed Madison's picture on her mantle. As she was about to sit down, the doorbell rang. Mrs. Kingsley stated that she would be right back and went to answer the door. It was Alondra.

Alondra apologized for dropping by while she had a guest. She then looked at the car and stated that it looks like MacKenzie's car. Mrs. Kingsley motioned for her to come in. When she stepped in there she was. MacKenzie was sitting on the couch. Alondra's heart started to race and she stepped back when MacKenzie looked and realized that she was there. Before MacKenzie could say a word, Alondra began to apologize. "MacKenzie I am so sorry. I never thought Dr. Morgan would do what she did to you." "Did you recommend me to be a surrogate mother for Dr. Morgan?" MacKenzie asked. "Yes, but I was joking. I told her that since you were not getting married, she should ask you, but then you announced your engagement so I figured she just forgot about it" said Alondra. "Alondra, when did I say I was willing to be a surrogate for anyone? Did you and I ever have that conversation?" Alondra just stood there in silence. "The fact that you and I never had a conversation about me being a surrogate mother makes what you are saying absolutely ridiculous.

I would ask you to tell me the truth, but I wouldn't believe you anyway. Please know that the thing that hurts the most is that I thought we were friends. Almost like sisters, but you betrayed me. You looked me in my face knowing what was happening and you never said a word. Friends don't do that. They tell you the truth. But then again, I guess we weren't friends, were we?" "No, I guess we weren't" says Alondra with a hint of anger. At that statement MacKenzie stood up. Alondra stepped back behind Mrs. Kingsley. Mrs. Kingsley turned to Alondra and stated that she was very disappointed in what she had done and that she needed to go to police and tell the truth. Alondra was reminded of how her life was spared when she had the accident with Joshua and that she knew that the Lord had not delivered her from such a horrible situation in order for to do such an evil act against someone else. "If you do not repent for what you have done and do the right thing by MacKenzie then how can you ever expect to be forgiven?" Alondra broke down crying. She began to speak to MacKenzie again, but this time she had a humble attitude. "MacKenzie, I swear to you that I didn't think Dr. Morgan would take me seriously. When I realized that she had, it was too late. I had given information about where you and Preston were honeymooning. When she came back to Seattle and told me what she had done, I didn't believe her at first. Then I realized that she was serious. I tried to convince her that she had to tell you what she had done, but she refused. When I told her that I would tell and go the police, she said that she would implicate me as an accomplice. I had to keep quiet. I was afraid to go to jail and of losing your friendship." "And how did that work out for you?" I asked. "Alondra, I will forgive you because the Lord says that I have to forgive you if I want to be forgiven when I sin. But don't get it twisted, you and I are done. Don't call me, tweet me, nothing. Mrs. Kingsley I thank you for your hospitality and what you tried to do for us, but after this there is no way I would ever trust her. Our relationship is beyond repair. Take care. See you at church Sunday." I gave Mrs. Kingsley a kiss and walked toward the door. Just then Alondra, now crying, stated again that she was sorry. I paused briefly. I then continued walking. I turned the doorknob and walked out of the house.

Mrs. Kingsley looked at a teary-eyed Alondra, and said, "Give her time. She's angry and she's hurting. You can't just say I'm sorry and think that it will instantly fix what has happened. Only time will allow her to truly forgive you. And she will, but not before she is ready. She knows that she has to forgive you because unforgiveness eats away at your very soul. Only she and the Lord knows when it will happen. Until that time comes, keep praying…and stay out her way. "